WORTH THE CHANCE

LAKE SPARK SERIES
BOOK 2

EVEY LYON

LAKE SPARK SERIES

Worth the Risk

Worth the Chance

Worth the Wait

Copyright © 2023 by Evey Lyon

Written and published by: Evey Lyon (EH Lyon)

Edited by: Contagious Edits

Cover design: Okay Creations

All rights reserved.

No part of this book may be reproduced in any form or by any electronic or mechanical means. Including information storage and retrieval systems, without written permission from the author, except for the use of brief quotations in a book review.

This book is a work of fiction. The names, characters, places, and incidents are products of the writer's imagination and used fictitiously and are not to be perceived as real. Any resemblance to persons, venues, events, businesses are entirely coincidental.

The author acknowledges the trademark status and trademark owners of various products referenced in this work of fiction, which have been used without permission. The publication/use of these trademarks is not authorized, associated with, or sponsored by the trademark owner.

This book is U.S. copy registered and further protected under international copyright laws.

ABOUT

April can't stand baseball star Spencer Crews, yet his proposition is the biggest curveball of his career...

Making a certain kind of video with my enemy—who happens to be everyone's favorite baseball player—was not my proudest moment, but I blame the alcohol or maybe Spencer's smirk three seconds before our clothes ended up on the floor for our one-night mistake. He said he deleted the video which is why I didn't expect the jerk to interrupt my date a few months later to break the news that we have a problem. His solution is for us to avoid the press by staying at his lake house to hide away, and I stupidly agree.

The next thing I know, I have two tiny eyes staring at me.

Yep, I discover Spencer is secretly a hot single dad to a cute little girl. And that's not the only twist because the small town by the lake seems to bring us closer—all of us. Spencer's and my arguments fizzle out, and our looks grow longer. We talk like it matters, and we study one another's bodies. It feels like we are lost in our own little world. And in the end, I'm not sure if it's Spencer or me trying to convince us that we may just be worth the chance...

Spencer and April bring the banter and steam in this enemies-to-lovers, single-dad, and completely swoon worthy forced-proximity story. Worth the Chance is book two in the standalone interconnected Lake Spark series. For lovers of small-town romance with a touch of sports.

APRIL

Plié, arabesque, jeté. *And* champagne spills over the edge of my glass.

Oh well. Another sip.

I gaze at the half-eaten tier of strawberry shortcake that is calling my name over there on the table. I would have done the icing a little differently, but who am I to criticize the award-winning inn in this little town of Lake Spark, Illinois?

I'm just the friend who had her fiancé leave her, and now I'm the twenty-six-year-old woman who left her job in accounting because, well, it wasn't for me. With that consideration, I grab hold of the near-empty bottle of champagne in my left hand and pour another glass.

Looking around me as I move, I reflect on the fact that I am alone in an empty private dining room at the Dizzy Duck Inn. A pool of pink confetti crunches between my bare toes, as my new heels were killing me, so I took them off after all the guests left. We may have gone a little overboard with the baby shower decorations, but it isn't often that your best friend is having a baby with your uncle/godfather.

To add to the pressure, everyone wanted an invite since he

is the one and only Hudson Arrows, football coach extraordinaire. But we kept it low-key and classy. My mom, my cousin Drew, and I arranged the baby shower—well, more party because it was a team dad and team mom event. I'm happy I could do this for Piper. After all, we had a bit of a falling out when I discovered she was sneaking around with my uncle, but we're all good now. Because even a fool could see they are perfect for each other.

Fifth position, assemblé, back to fifth.

It's been years since I've done ballet. I let my feet gravitate into their own dance, the knee-length teal dress swaying out perfectly and making me want to watch the fabric flow. I'm not sure why in this moment dance is calling to me, but someone, literally, *is* calling out to me.

"April." That tone fills me with dread.

My body tightens as that voice satisfies my disdain quota for the year. Exactly what I needed tonight; baseball royalty rolling in. "Spencer."

Ugh, he chuckles under his breath. It's irritating because of how it is enticing, *if* I were the kind of woman who finds arrogant baseball players attractive. And I. Am. Not.

Spencer appears in my peripheral vision as he walks right past me to grab another bottle of champagne from the bucket of nearly melted ice. Damn it, I missed that bottle. He gets to work on breaking the foil.

He's wearing dark blue jeans, dress shoes, and a shirt that only accentuates those upper arm muscles that earn him millions. God, his cologne is a little strong today, and his new haircut of short summer length just seems a little overboard for his sandy-brown hair.

"Where's the tutu?" he asks, which means he must have spied on me in my little dance escape.

That's it. I feel my face forming a sneer as I slowly turn to face him. "Do you not have to go home? I mean, thank you for gracing us with your presence at the baby shower, but I feel the ground turning cold which must mean your stellar personality is freezing the earth."

He scoffs a laugh as he perches against the table, and with his brown eyes set on me, I notice how the shade of green of his shirt complements his eyes, which is beside the point. "I love that you dislike me so much. It's not often I share mutual feelings with a woman."

"Gag. Don't put me on a list with your gazillion skanks."

"Wouldn't dream of it. Plus, gaggers don't get a place on my list. I'm more a swallow-and-smile kind of guy." I would literally throw up if it wasn't for the fact there is a hint of sarcasm in his voice, the saving grace from this horrendous conversation.

I roll my eyes. "I knew there was a reason I avoided you all day."

"Nah, you did that because I bring out the worst in you and you wanted to be on good behavior for Piper and Hudson."

I really want to throttle him. Good behavior my ass. I'm not Ms. Prim and Proper.

Pop. The cork goes flying, but neither one of us seems to notice.

He continues to speak. "I wanted to drink today, avoid the last of the construction on my house, and maybe have a spa day tomorrow with a hot masseuse before I head deep into baseball season, so I'm staying here tonight. Hudson texted that he thought he forgot some gift in here, some silver duck or something, so that's why I am submitting myself to your presence again."

My eyes bug out. "You live literally four miles from here." He's my uncle's and Piper's next-door neighbor. I met him through my uncle Hudson at a BBQ, and I always saw him at other events. It was an instant dislike, mostly because Spencer possesses a smug smirk that I just want to…

He pours himself a glass. "And? Foxes on the road this time of a day can be a killer."

I snort a laugh, because as ridiculous as it sounds, it's true because Lake Spark is surrounded by woods.

Offering him my glass, he cocks a brow before filling my glass up too. "What's your excuse?"

"I don't live in Lake Spark, and I didn't want to drive back to Chicago today. So, alcohol and a soft hotel bed it is." I struggle to give a tight, closed-mouth smile.

He pauses before finishing his task of filling my glass to the brim. "Hopefully they put us on opposite ends of the hotel then."

"Oh, wow, we agree on something," I counter. I take another sip and realize I should pace myself around this man.

In a bizarre twist, I trust the man in a "he would keep me safe" kind of way, but I don't trust… myself around Spencer Crews, star pitcher of the Bluelights.

"You know there was a stop sign," he mentions.

Aggravation seeps through me that he wants to go down memory lane, starting with the time I was arriving at Spencer and my uncle's street once and nearly had a car accident.

"Yes, there was. You probably didn't see it because of the bush by the sign. So I was right with my traffic skills, and I had the right of way."

"No, you didn't," he insists.

"You nearly hit my car in the process!"

He tilts his head to the side. "A little dramatic."

"Really? And what about my uncle's BBQ a while back? What is your explanation for your asshole tendency there?" I slam the glass onto a table.

"Oh, that's easy. You walked around all holier than thou, and your boyfriend at the time is the kind of jackass that will cheat on his future wife and only look out for himself."

The air in the room evaporates, and he instantly seems to regret his words, as his cocky demeanor fades into almost remorse. He's close with Hudson and Piper, which means they must update him on my life.

A twinge below my heart ignites as my eyes fall to the floor. "Well… joke is on me then, right?" I say softly.

Spencer steps closer. "I'm sorry. That was… out of line."

I peer up. "It's the truth, isn't it? If only I had known then what you so wisely figured out. I mean, I could have saved myself an entire engagement." I fake a laugh.

I walk past him and straight to the window overlooking Lake Spark; the sun is setting which casts an orange and purple hue across the sky.

Time seems to still as I try to forget the fact that I would've had a wedding coming up if it weren't for Jeff deciding that I'm not what he needs.

A tap on my shoulder causes me to look down, and I see a glass of champagne held out in a firm hand. "Here."

"Did you add poison?" I wonder.

"Nah, to have me in your company is probably agonizing enough."

I straighten my posture and take the glass. "Right. We irritate each other."

The corner of his mouth curves, and I seem to notice the five-o'clock shadow around his lips more than I care to admit.

"So, what's with the dancing earlier?" He looks into his glass.

"Old habit."

A long breath escapes his mouth before he leans against

the window and seems to be casting his gaze on me. "You were a ballerina?"

"Somewhat."

His eyes go wide, as if he's waiting for more. "Care to elaborate?"

"No," I answer bluntly. In truth, it's nothing special. I only danced until I was fifteen, then turned in my point shoes for the swim team. I wasn't very good at that either.

Spencer bites his inner cheek before his jaw slides side to side. "Do you always act like a child, or do I just bring out the best in you?"

My hand finds my hip. "Forgive me for having a zero-tolerance policy for jerks who play baseball."

"Come on, give me some credit. I'm an MVP jerk who plays baseball with any team willing to pay for my arm."

I set my glass down, and my hands fly into the air. "See? Your arrogance is something else."

"Confidence is a good thing to have, April."

"I have confidence," I say, quick to defend myself.

He doesn't answer but instead shakes his head subtly, as if he's amused. "You stopped dancing the moment I came into the room."

"Because you dampen the mood with your pure existence."

The corners of his mouth twist as everything I say only seems to entertain him. "Well, on that note, I'll let you be." He propels his body off the window that he was leaning against and glides his way across the room with the champagne bottle hanging from one hand and his lips sipping from the glass in his other hand.

I don't say anything, just watch him leave with derision written all over my face. When the door closes behind him, relief fills me, but I can't seem to look away from the exit, as if he may just walk back in, and my eyes linger longer than needed on the door.

———

I'M SLIGHTLY dizzy yet way too sober to be knocking on Spencer's hotel room door. I don't bang with elegance. I thought when he left an hour ago that I wouldn't have to see him again until he shows up on a TV screen because of a baseball game.

"Spencer, open up."

It takes only a few seconds before he complies. "Fuck, what in the world? I was recording a video of my arm flexes for my trainer."

Gah, sounds like the perfect recipe for his egotistical ways. But never mind, I have bigger problems.

I barge in his direction, brushing past him into the room. "You have something that's mine." I pivot sharply to give him a death stare.

He walks slowly back into the room with the door clicking shut, while he drags the back of his fingers along his chin before a sinister smirk forms. "Is that so?" he rasps.

My hands land on my hips. "The hotel staff accidentally delivered the leftover cake to your room. Please, can I have the cake?"

His eyes squint at me, like I've said something crazy. "You came here for cake?"

"Yes! I wanted a piece. They said they would bring it up to my room."

"Fine. But I keep the champagne." He tips his nose in the direction behind me, indicating where the cake is sitting on a table.

I march on over and grab the fork to dig right in. Okay, maybe I am a little tipsy, and food is my refuge.

"God, this is so good." I admit that I moan as I suck on the fork.

"You know my mouth may have been on that fork, but I'm sure that's just your fantasy, right?"

I glance over my shoulder to find him sitting on the edge of his bed with arms crossed and a cunning grin.

"The only way I like your mouth is when it is taped shut."

His eyes grow bold. "Kinky. I like that."

I growl at his way of taunting. "Stop trying to piss me off more than normal."

"What am I possibly doing now?"

"Y-you… you're trying to egg me on by thinking I have some crush on you or some bullshit like that. I'm not other women, I don't care who you are, and I certainly do not find you attractive. Besides, I'm not even your type."

Why, April? Why did I even say that?

He only hums a sound, followed by a long pause. I feel like he is studying me. "You're right. My type is overconfident chicks who don't stop dancing on my account."

"Fuck you. I didn't stop because I'm not confident."

Oh no, we're bickering again. Feels like a flashback to the time Piper and Hudson had us over for dinner and they had to change the seating arrangements between salad and steak courses to ensure Spencer and I had distance between us.

Spencer smiles to himself and stands up to grab his glass of champagne.

Damn. Looks like he nearly finished the bottle.

He takes a drink then offers me the glass that I stupidly accept, as if I need to replenish my liquid intake.

"You seem a little edgy. Is it me?" he pretends to be concerned.

I swear I snarl at him. "Like, I totally understand why you are single and ready to mingle. It's impossible to enjoy even a millisecond with you."

"Mmm, I care to disagree. I'm just currently stuck in the proximity of an uptight woman."

I instantly act and splash the glass of champagne in his face. "I'm anything but."

When his face stills and his tongue darts out to taste the alcohol on the corner of his mouth, I realize my error. My jaw drops open, and I can't believe I just did that.

He uses the back of his hand to wipe away a few drops from his cheek as his eyes darken before he gives me a pointed look. "What the hell."

My shock fades into a smile that wants to spread.

He steps closer, and I don't move.

"Unpredictable. I'm unpredictable," I declare because inside I'm acting this way for reasons that have nothing to do with Spencer, but I don't want him to know what's going on in my mind.

But before I can process the elation I feel that I may just be everything my former fiancé thought I wasn't, I feel something gooey hit my cheek.

I blink and realize that Spencer reached over and grabbed cake with two fingers before he smothered it on my face.

He's standing far too close to me with a satisfied look. "Oops."

I touch the sticky icing with my palm, only to quickly shove his hand away, but he is quick to circle his fingers around my wrists. "Don't start something you can't finish," he warns.

"I'm very capable of finishing, thank you very much," I snipe back.

His look turns to a mix of warning and interest. "I bet," he rasps.

"Please do."

I break my wrists free from his impressive grip that is equal parts gentle yet proof of his career as a pitcher.

But the moment I'm free, his arm circles around my middle, and my response is to grip his shirt with my fingers. I feel like something is combusting inside of me, a form of hysteria that has me drawn to his eyes, then darting my vision down to his mouth before snapping my attention back to his piercing gaze.

And I'm not sure who in this moment is more eager to take a chance on a wager.

2
SPENCER

A FEW MONTHS LATER

I peer up from my phone as I approach the restaurant. I've heard teammates rave about it, but that's not why I'm here. It's the end of the baseball season, or rather our batter struck out at a key moment running up to the World Series, so our team is out early, and hopefully, the batter is getting traded for next season.

I was finishing up some meetings with my agent and publicist when I got the message that added another complication to my life.

I should be in my car with music on full blast while I drive back to Lake Spark. Instead, I'm walking down a sidewalk in downtown Chicago with a few people noticing me, but I have no intention to smile and sign autographs. It's not because I'm an ass, it's because I'm on a mission. Okay, I'm not a fan of people either.

Opening the restaurant's door, I glance at the screen on my phone and see my mother sent me a message with a picture. It causes my lips to tug, but my mouth doesn't commit to a full smile as the message is a reminder of another life that I keep under wraps.

Arriving at the hostess station, a brunette smiles at me and flicks her hair behind her shoulder. Her eyes fill with recognition. "Hi. Welcome, can I get you a seat?" I can tell she is a supporter of my career—or wallet—by the eagerness of her voice and overdone smile.

I swipe my sunglasses off my face and tuck them into the pocket of my black button-down. "No, thanks. I'm here to meet someone."

"Oh. Nobody mentioned you would be joining us tonight, but we are happy to have you here." Her smile doesn't falter. She seems keen.

I scan the busy room. It's 7pm which means those who worked all day are now carrying on their evening with business dinners. That was never my scene. I'm more of a "throw back beer with the guys" type of man.

"It's kind of a surprise," I mention, as I now search the room, determined.

Ah, bingo. I spot her.

Wearing a black dress and hoop earrings, it kind of suits her, but I don't think about it for long. She is next to the window and sitting across from a guy, wasn't planning on that, but this day is already hell enough, so what's one more obstacle?

"Found her. If you don't mind, could you send over a scotch on the rocks and make it a double? Thanks, you're a doll." Before the hostess can answer, I'm walking at a fast pace to the table by the window.

I'm not in baseball season which means I don't need to think twice about drinking alcohol. In season, I stay off the hard stuff and only have a beer if it's a few days before a game. I haven't committed years to the sport to throw it away to a bad practice or game because I'm hungover.

Assessing the scene, I sense that I'm witnessing a date, clearly.

Grabbing a chair from a nearby table before I reach my destination, I pull it up just in time to hear the mystery guy talking about anesthesia, and April is politely listening until she does a double take when I appear in her vision.

"Spencer!" April shrieks when her eyes land on me, obviously surprised by my presence. Her brown eyes grow big, almost in wonder that I'm in front of her. And hell, I could think of many other people who I would rather be sitting in front of right now. This woman detests me.

And in a moment where logic left me, I found her bratty ways attractive enough.

"Oh, hey there! Am I interrupting? Surely, I'm not interrupting." My cocky smirk is out in full force.

The man who could use a steak or two looks at me peculiarly. "Aren't you Spencer Crews?"

"I am. And you must be...?"

He answers me in awe, "Ted."

"Ted's a doctor, a cardiologist actually," April pipes in, and I'm instantly amused that she feels the need to try and level the guy up.

Now I have to grin. "You know, I think I read once that cardiologists have like, I don't know, the highest rate of heart attacks or burnout due to stress, plus long work weeks. Must be grueling for your future wife." No clue why I decided to highlight this stranger's faults to April.

April's face is fuming, and I can tell that I've hit a nerve. "As opposed to baseball players who retire by thirty?"

"Are you retiring? Shit, now the Bluelights are going to suck," Ted adds his commentary.

"Spencer lives next door to my uncle," she explains.

I turn my attention back to the guy. "So, you are April's new boyfriend?" I internally question why I'm curious.

He grabs a piece of bread from the basket. "It's actually our first date."

"Oh, wonderful. And here I am interrupting." I lean back just as the hostess hands me my drink. Perfect timing, as I could use the liquid encouragement right now for what's about to go down. But my confident look doesn't fade.

"How the hell did you know I was here?" April asks, clearly agitated.

I tilt my head gently to the side. "Your love of cameras."

Her eyes fill with recognition as they don't blink, and since her dress is hanging low at her tits, then I notice her breath pick up.

I'm quick to clarify. "You posted on your social media story a photo of your cocktail, and the logo of the place was on the napkin. You really should work on safety first."

Her hands nearly claw the tablecloth. "And why the hell would you be looking at my social media?"

"Do you two need a moment? I feel like I'm missing something," Ted says, but neither April nor I look at him, as we are too busy in a standoff.

"How about I just steal this pocketful of sunshine away for a moment?" I suggest to Ted.

April's body stiffens, but she gives the doctor a tight smile. "Just a minute, I'll be right back, and then we can order dinner."

Ted gives us an odd look. "Oh, uhm, sure."

Clearly, their date wasn't going so great anyways.

April grabs my arm. "Two minutes," she grinds out.

She pulls me out of my seat, and I follow, only I don't like being towed along. I step forward and place my hand on her lower back to take the lead, for a second, I appreciate the fact that her dress is a little snug around her hips.

I lean in and nearly murmur, "Don't you have a sweater or something?"

She flashes me a death stare. "Why?"

"I just think Hudson would appreciate that I'm watching out for his niece and ensuring Dr. Stress keeps his gaze appropriate," I attempt to justify.

But fuck me, Hudson may kill me for what is transpiring and what I did with his niece who is his goddaughter and wife's best friend. I should have probably thought about the rules of our friendship a little more, but then again, Hudson is laid back and even attempted to push me in April's direction once or twice, like at the baby shower a few months back. I'm not blind.

The moment we are at an empty spot near the bar, she shakes me away and turns her full attention to me.

"No sweater." Her tone is clipped. "Which, by the way, it's a little late to be concerned with manners that my uncle would approve of." Her brows arch; she's in a feisty mood. "Our first contact in months, and I already feel like knowing you is a regret. Now explain why the hell I am being graced by your presence this evening?"

My lips quirk out as we both take a beat to look at each other. I haven't seen April since that night a few months ago. Her blonde locks are in waves around her face; it looks natural, but I get the feeling she put in the extra effort with her hair tonight. I guess her skin is tanner too. I heard she went to Italy for a little while in place of the honeymoon that she had hoped to go on. Piper told me when I ran into her on my driveway, which makes me wonder if Piper knows...

"Does anyone know about—"

"Hush your mouth!" She is quick to interrupt and steps

closer, a sort of warning as she nervously searches the room. "And what? Admit my mistake? God no."

I debate my words for a second, but I can only chuckle nervously. "Okay, well, we have a tiny problem."

Her brows raise in curiosity, and I see concern spread across her face. "What do you mean?"

I look over her shoulder to ensure nobody can hear and lean closer to whisper, "The video."

Her entire body tenses, and concern is replaced with fear. I notice because she peers her eyes up, causing our breaths to mingle, as we are close in proximity. "The video?"

I scratch my cheek. "You know, the one we accidentally made while we were—"

Her palm lands against my chest to stop me from continuing, and it creates space between us. God, this woman touches me like she knows exactly which spot awakens a feral need inside me. It's downright infuriating.

"Do *not* say the words," she nearly barks then throws on a small fake smile when the barman walks by our spot to collect a glass.

The moment he passes, our eyes lock, and I see the fear, but it's laced with… heat. I know it's there.

"You deleted the video. I saw you delete the video." Her voice has panic in it.

Licking my lips, I'm about to bite the bullet. "I did… but I kind of…" It's dragging out.

Her nails sharply dig into my arm. "Kind of what?"

"I forgot that it autosaved to my cloud."

"Of course, it saved to your cloud. What kind of person doesn't know that you need to delete it from your phone *and* the cloud. Fuck." Disbelief is strong in her tone. She steps back, and her hand fans her face as she is clearly trying to calm down. "I knew you were trouble. Holy hell, this is…"

I lean against the bar to watch her, but admittedly, guilt does ping inside of me. "I'm sorry."

Her eyes draw a line up to my own again. "Wait, why are you telling me this?"

I'm quick to straighten my posture and land my hands on her arms to have her full attention. "I was hacked, and I'm not quite sure what will come of it."

"Oh my God!" She is about to melt down. "This isn't happening. No. Nope. This. Is. Not. Happening."

Closing our distance, I pull her to me, as if I'm her protector, but in truth, I'll be damned if anyone leaks the video. I have my own personal reasons why it can't happen, but April is still the major factor. "My publicist and lawyer are on it. I don't think it will ever see the light of day. This kind of thing happens to my teammates all the time. We just need to stay on the down-low until it's solved."

"What the fuck is with my life? Exactly what I need now. I mean, my lawyer mother will be so proud that her daughter made a hate-sex tape with her favorite baseball player," she bites out.

"I'm her favorite player?" I can't help but smirk proudly.

Her eyes bug out at me. "Not the time for your stupid arrogance. Holy shit, this is bad. Like, *really* bad." Her hand finds her forehead. "I mean, we didn't even intentionally mean to make it."

True. We were kind of at each other's throats before ripping our clothes off happened, and then we went at it like two wild animals. By the time I realized that my phone video was on while it sat on the docking station, it only seemed to encourage us more.

"They can tell it's more me than you. Besides, I won't let the leak happen." I hear the sincerity in my voice, a sort of possessiveness that I feel, like I want to owe it to her.

"How are you going to do that, Spencer?" She attempts to breathe out a calming breath.

My head lolls slightly at an angle, and I feel my face strain because if I didn't know she enjoyed my dick, I'd be worried she may just hit me in the balls in a second. "It's best if we're off the radar for a bit. I was heading back to Lake Spark, but I think you should also stay there for a while."

"What?"

"It's better to tackle this when we are away from the city. We need to be near each other to stay updated, plus if shit really hits the fan, then it's easier to spin that you are a long-term…"

Her finger flies up to stop me. "Don't say that either."

"Girlfriend? I mean, we don't need to fake a relationship, just if the press somehow finds us, then it looks slightly better, and they'll be more sympathetic."

April cocks a brow. "Finds us?"

I swipe a hand across my jaw. "I mean, I hate suggesting it, because I can only imagine that hell resembles something similar to living with you, but you should stay at my place until the dust settles."

She throws her hands up in the air to demonstrate that she has given up on this conversation. "Roommates. Just fantastic." This woman seethes cynicism flawlessly. "How long do you think this will take?"

"Two weeks maybe. Look, I'm sorry, truly I am, but I think it's for the best that you tell Dr. McLoser to take a hike since there was no way you were enjoying it anyhow, then go home and pack your bags."

"Hey, Ted could be a real contender if you didn't interrupt." She sounds almost offended.

I look at her skeptically. "You looked bored until I showed up."

Right on cue, Dr.McLoser taps on Piper's arm. "Hey, the hospital called, and I'm needed."

"Really?" I throw out my doubt.

"Hey, man, could I get your autograph before I go? I'm such a fan." Ted looks at me, excited.

April shakes her head, as if she has nothing left to lose.

I shoot him a fuck-off grin. "You know, I don't do autographs after dinner time. Work-life balance, am I right?"

"Oh, yeah, sure, I totally get that." He tries to save himself and then turns his attention to April "I guess I'll…"

She rolls her eyes. "It's fine. We don't need to pretend we'll call one another. Have a good night."

"You too."

Jesus, that was painful to watch.

I wait for the doctor to disappear and for April, who now looks defeated, to say something, but she doesn't. Instead, her shoulders fall before she plops herself on a free bar stool. She raises her finger to grab the barman's attention.

Stepping closer to her, I lean against the bar as she asks for two shots of vodka. Yikes, this is bad, as that's a bold order.

"April," I say her name with firmness, but I need her attention again.

An audible breath escapes as she twirls on the stool to focus on me.

"Are you okay with the plan?" God, I wish I had another option.

"I have no choice. So, shacking up with you it is."

Huh, I thought this would require a little more debate.

My jaw flexes as I ponder that thought before it registers that by letting April stay at my house, I'm letting her into the parts of my personal life that not many people know. I require a lot of trust when it comes to my life outside of baseball, but

April staying at my place is the only way. I need to chance it, and a part of me doesn't seem to be second-guessing about letting April in.

The shots of vodka show up, and we each take one. She doesn't hesitate and downs it.

I tap my drink on her now-empty glass that she set on the bar. "Cheers."

Her head makes a sharp turn in my direction, and she narrows her eyes in on me. "How do you know they can tell it's more you than me?"

I scoff a sound instead of giving her words.

"Did you watch the video?" she wonders.

It isn't anger, nerves, or fear that is in her voice. It's almost an acknowledgment that there is something underlying if I did.

I've been caught out because I may have watched a scene or two. "How could I not? Hate sex brings out the best performance, which means we were award-worthy, since we might've actually looked like two people who passionately want each other."

I stand and decide this is my moment to leave her.

We'll have enough time to soak in our situation when she is under my roof.

3
APRIL

I want to see the video. That can't be a bad idea, right? I should demand to see the proof of our little escapade. It's my right.

I swing my legs out of my small SUV, and I groan at the fact that I just pulled up to Spencer's house. He lives on a cul-de-sac with two other houses, one of which is Piper and Hudson's, and the other belongs to a hockey player. All the houses deserve a spot in an architecture magazine, plus they all back onto the lake.

Rage fills me as I walk to the back of my car to grab my suitcases because I'm here for God knows how long.

As I'm opening the trunk, I hear a familiar voice that may just be my saving grace in this situation.

"April?" Piper asks as she approaches with baby Gracie in one of those wrap things. Despite being sleep-deprived, Piper always looks put-together, and her brown hair is up in a bun that looks messy in an on-purpose fashionable way.

I look at her as I swing my suitcase out, and my new beagle Pickles jumps out onto the driveway too.

"Oh, hey."

"Uhm. Think you parked at the wrong house. I wasn't expecting you. I mean, it's great, I just need to change the sheets in the guest room." She looks affectionately at her daughter who is also my cousin. I know my uncle isn't around because there is an away game this week.

It dawns on me that this situation took such a fast spin that I haven't updated Piper on the latest.

I bite the bullet and bring my hand to my hip, knowing there is an awkward look plastered on my face. "I'm not here to stay with you."

"Right… then what are you here for?" She seems confused.

I smile tightly then bite my lip. "I'm… going to *temporarily* live with Spencer." That was painful to say, and I cover my face in near shame.

"As in my neighbor? The guy you hate? Wait, the guy who you actually call the asshole baseball player?"

"Yep." I pop the P with my lips.

"Why?" she asks blankly.

I laugh nervously. "Fun story. Or *not*. Remember your baby shower?" God, I'm going to admit this, but it's better if she knows the details, because the only plus of this situation is that I get to hang with my bestie more due to her close proximity.

"Of course." Piper smiles because I'm sure it is a great memory for her. "But what about the baby shower?"

I use my fingers to indicate size. "I might have made a teensy-weensy mistake with Spencer, and the man forgot to use the delete button. So, I need to hide out here in case the press figures it out." I'm speaking at the speed of light.

Piper's blank look fades to shock. "Oh my God!"

Pickles makes a whimpering sound, as if he is agreeing with Piper. Thank goodness I adopted him when I got back from my Italy vacation; I could use a therapy dog right about now.

I give a weak wave and smile to Piper. "Howdy, neighbor."

"We are not telling Hudson the specifics of this," Piper states, still in shock.

"Please don't." I couldn't agree more.

"Oh, hey there, roomie," I hear Spencer call out as he appears to walk slowly with a swagger down his driveway.

My face turns stiff, and I hold up my middle finger in his direction, but my eyes stay fixed on Piper. I feel my nostrils flare before smiling sweetly at my friend. "You'll be my alibi if a hot baseball player turns up at the bottom of Lake Spark?"

Piper seems to be grinning. "I shouldn't highlight the fact that you just called him hot, should I?"

I grumble and wave her off as I start my march in the direction of the house, with my hound in tow. I vaguely hear Piper say, "See you soon." I am sure she flashes Spencer a smile because that man has everyone wrapped around his finger.

Spencer slows as we come face to face. "What's with the dog?"

"My ex hated dogs, so I lost the ex and gained a dog. Clearly a win. We are a package deal. You need me to stay here, then Pickles stays too." I shoot him a glare.

He responds by smirking. "Fine. Shall I get your suitcase?"

"It won't move itself." My eyes flick down to get a glance at his white t-shirt that hugs his muscles, and I see half of his tattoo on his chest by the v-neck. An anchor with tiny numbers along the outline of the shape; I know that because I've seen his entire body.

"Great, I get to live with children," I hear him mumble. Creases form on my forehead that he said that plural, but I don't think too long.

Mostly because I'm mesmerized as I enter his home. He was working on this house for a long time. Everything is state-of-the-art and modern. An open staircase greets me, as does the one-room level with floor-to-ceiling windows. It's huge, and I don't know where to look. The living area, a dining area, then my eyes land on the kitchen.

I'm a little eager as I continue my journey to inspect the kitchen. This fridge is a dream, and is that a pizza oven? I think I've entered heaven. In Italy, I partook in cooking workshops every day, but my apartment in the city just doesn't suffice for some of the recipes, but this? I can literally stare at this all day.

This will be great.

I mean, don't, April, don't get a warm fuzzy feeling about this arrangement.

I turn to face Spencer, who has left the luggage by the stairs and followed me in my exploration. "Since I'm here, I might as well stay occupied and use the kitchen for my own enjoyment." I hear my attempt to cover my excitement.

"Sure." He scratches the back of his neck. "We may need to stock up on supplies. We can head to the general store if you want?"

My voice turns sickly sweet. "I would say I don't need your company, but I do need your credit card since this shall be an unexpected all-expenses-paid trip, because the reason I am here…" My voice turns full of venom. "Is because you forgot to use the damn delete button on your cloud!"

His satisfied smirk is unaffected. "Fair point, but it did take two to make it."

Ugh, he's right. I soften a smidgen and blow out a confirming breath.

"Do you need me to show you where you can work or something during the day?"

"No. I'm currently unemployed, on a sabbatical, trying to figure out life, yadda yadda, whatever you want to call it. I made a deal with my old company when I left, so I can weigh out my options for a little. I'm about to finish a nutrition course, but that's online, and I'm practicing recipes."

"Hmm, I could see you as a nutritionist." He walks past me to the fridge to grab a soda. "Want a drink?"

"No, it's okay. But I should get some water for Pickles." We both look at my dog who is standing in the middle of the kitchen panting.

Spencer angles his head to study my pet. "Does his eye always twitch?"

"Yes. I adopted him from the shelter. He's older, so nobody wanted him, but he is a big softie and a good dog."

To my surprise, Spencer grabs a bowl and fills it with water. He is already confusing me with his effort. I thought he would tell me to get it myself.

He sets the dish down. "You can have any of the guest rooms."

I stare at him with a neutral face. I thought for sure he would take the opportunity to reference that night, but he doesn't, and I'm not sure why that disappoints me. Shaking off the thought, I get us back on track.

"I'll take the room farthest from you. It will be less enticing to strangle you in your sleep."

He rubs his face in aggravation. "Your maturity level needs work."

"Well, you do bring out the best in me." I plaster on a fake smile before walking past him. When I reach my suitcase at the bottom of the stairs, I clear my throat, indicating for him to carry my bag. I'm going to make the man work because we are in this mess because of him. Plus, seeing his muscles flex *may* be a bonus.

Spencer scoffs and reluctantly follows me until he purposely leans over to grab the handle and grazes my body in the process. He is doing that on purpose, right? I mean, his shoulder touches my arm, and the smell of his freshly shampooed hair hits my nose. Something inside of me feels heightened.

"Remind me to find my handcuffs in case you get out of line," he mentions before heading up the steps.

Leaving me to picture the thought in my head.

OF COURSE, Spencer speeds along the road to the general store. I guess what man wouldn't when you have a Jaguar like this?

"When is your lawyer updating you on the situation?" I ask as I look out the window.

"I have a call with Celeste tomorrow. I think she works with your mother, as they are in the same firm." He focuses on the road with his hand on the wheel.

My lips roll in from the thought of my mother finding out about the video. "Yeah, she does. Since I know she has client confidentiality then I won't worry about her telling my mother. But make no mistake, this goes down as the worst one-night stand in history, hands down."

"Let's maybe not get into it while we approach the sharp turns around the lake."

"Fair point."

He glances to his side real quick, I see it in the corner of my eye. "I forget that Lake Spark is your family spot."

I smile to myself because it's true. "Well, I've been coming here for years. My mom and uncle always visited, and then Hudson bought his house, so Lake Spark became a frequent visit. Then my best friend decided to become his wife. I don't need a map for this area, as I'm here often enough."

"Good. I can just let you be and not worry about you getting lost in the woods or something."

I shoot him a glare. "Touching."

Arriving at the general store, I know it's anything but a basic stop. This place is a gourmet supermarket for all the people of Lake Spark who enjoy paying an arm and a leg for almond milk.

Spencer and I get out of the car, and I grab a cart that I pass on to Spencer.

"I need to get a few things," he says as we enter the store and land right in the produce area.

"I would assume so, as it's essential to living."

He stops the cart, causing me to stumble against it. Spencer's eyes turn stormy, and he steps closer, leaning in to mutter so only I can hear.

"Considering your fingers loved to dig into the shape of my ass, then I would really start coming up with better retorts. Speaking of coming, what was it…" He pretends to contemplate. "Oh yeah, three times, of which two of those times were around my big cock."

His fingers tuck a strand of my hair behind my ear as he pulls away, and just like a bubble popping, he grabs a bunch of bananas, as if the last five seconds didn't happen. "Oh, look at that." He inspects the fruit. "Just a little too small to compare, but hey, we need our potassium, right?" He throws them into the baby seat of the cart and starts to push again.

I bite my tongue and swallow any words that are fighting to come out.

"Should we split up? You know, divide and conquer?" I suggest in a normal tone.

"Sure, I need to find the jars of apple sauce."

What the hell? I don't see this guy eating apple sauce, but I don't want to carry on this conversation.

"Fine."

He leaves the cart with me, and I begin my moments of solitude, throwing in items that look good, with no thought process. I figure I will just scrape something together when I'm in the kitchen.

Avocados for sure because that is essential. The unrefrigerated oat milk also goes into the cart. Throw in some boxes of granola. Hitting up the international food aisle and going crazy on sauces, I get an idea to make tortellini from scratch. Since they have a pasta maker on sale, I don't think twice. Realizing I need fresh cheese, I head to the deli counter, lost in my own world.

But when I grab my little paper number from the machine for my turn, I freeze when I hear a familiar voice talking to two other guys, and not in the "oh joy, an acquaintance" way. This is "dread and throw me under a bus" kind of way.

Turning to face my demise, I see Jett, my ex-fiancé's brother. Shit, I forgot his brother comes to Lake Spark often for "corporate retreats." It's how I met Jeff, on the Lake Spark beach one weekend. And yes, their parents should be questioned for naming their kids Jett and Jeff.

"April?" He looks at me.

I wiggle a few fingers. "Hi." There is no excitement in my tone, but I attempt to offer a friendly look.

"I-I... well, uhm, it's good to see you." He is trying to be polite as he looks awkwardly at the two guys next to him. They all look like preppy accountants who cheat on their girlfriends. "This is April."

"*The* April?" one of the guys asks, then his face turns cartoonish.

"Yep. Jeff's ex," I confirm. "What a coincidence. What brings you three here? A weekend getaway?" I raise my brows.

Jett awkwardly scratches the back of his neck as his jaw flexes. "We are kind of checking out the area for a bachelor party later in the year. Surprising the groom."

"Bet you are."

"It's Jeff," one of the guys mentions.

I try to hold it together, but I want to throw up, as this is news to me. Rage fills me, and pure outright hurt. I was ditched, and clearly, someone moved on, ready for marriage in record time. I have no clue what my face gives away or what to say. It's been a year since Jeff broke off our engagement, and even though I now know he would have made a horrible husband, I wanted him to have a miserable year or two.

But the problem wasn't us, or him, it was me. I'm the reason that we had no future.

I feel my throat burn, as if I want to scream or cry. Humiliation is what's crossing my mind while everyone waits for me to react. I can't hear or blink, I'm lost in how to respond.

An arm wraps around my middle, breaking my trance.

"There you are, baby." Spencer pulls me flush against his body, and his hot breath brushes along my jawline before he nuzzles his nose against my cheek. "Did you get everything we need for our dinner tonight?"

My mind now focuses on him and the fact my body seems to remember his touch. I think I might even relax slightly.

"Holy shit, it's Spencer Crews," one of the guys calls out.

Spencer keeps me in his hold and gives a hard look to the guy. "Yeah, but I kind of want to finish up our grocery store trip soon. Got a busy night planned with my girl."

My eyes draw a line to Spencer's face, and I swear I see a flicker of empathy that I both equally appreciate and hate.

He takes it up a notch and moves in, with his mouth landing near my neck. The feeling of his breath spreads against my skin. A flicker of a flashback of him doing this once before hits me, and my body curves into him in response. Then he places a kiss to the side of my neck with a little teeth action for good measure.

I softly gasp from the bite, but I play along. "Babe, I just needed to grab the cheese, then we can head home."

"You're living with him?" Jett asks, confused.

"Jett is the brother of my… ex," I mutter in explanation with a tight smile.

Spencer entwines his fingers with mine to hold my hand before looking to Jett. "Well, only unwise men give up another man's treasure." He tugs my hand. "Come on, I'm sure Sean behind the counter will toss us the…" Spencer flashes a persuasive grin to the college-aged guy in an apron behind the counter before turning to me to answer.

I'm in a daze from the last minute. "Oh, right, fresh parmesan and pecorino."

"Sounds delicious. Hope we actually make it to the main course this time."

My eyes blaze open, as he is laying it on a little thick.

Jett looks between us. "I… it was good seeing you."

"Yeah, same," I call out as he waves, and his minions follow as he walks away.

When the group of guys are out of our sight, my attention reverts back to Spencer who is biting his inner cheek.

"Isn't pecorino the same as parmesan?" He is attempting to ignore the fact of what he just did.

"I'm not a damsel in distress," I rasp because his poisonous spell is clearly affecting me.

His eyes look at my mouth and then back to my eyes. "Of course not."

Realizing we are still in an embrace, I push against his chest with my palms. "We should probably go."

"Good idea."

4
APRIL

That man is a curse.

In the last forty-eight hours, Spencer has brought nothing but bad luck to me.

I was silent on our way back to his house. In truth, my thoughts couldn't muster any words, as I was lost in what just happened over the last hour. If I'm honest with myself, I know it's because I feel I wasn't good enough for my ex, which only infuriates me. Then Spencer acted… chivalrous.

Following Spencer into his kitchen, we both carry groceries. He stalls when he sets the bags on the counter.

He tilts his head at different angles. "Your dog is lazy."

My eyes follow his line of sight to see Pickles in the same spot that we left him in before we went into town.

"He isn't lazy. He is just enjoying the finer things in life which is called relaxation. Don't be a hater on his life balance," I chide.

"As long as he doesn't destroy anything in the house, then he can enjoy his life of Zen."

I blow out a breath because I feel uneasy. I'm not quite sure what to do with this nervous energy.

"I'm sure you can handle this." I indicate to the groceries, knowing that I'm acting a smidgen too bitchy even for my standards, but it feels like a part that I need to keep playing.. "I'm going to go swim in the lake."

"It's early October?" Spencer questions.

"Cold water is good for the skin."

"Or you can just use the indoor swimming pool like a normal person."

Something ticks inside of me. It's his words, and Spencer has no idea.

Crossing my arms, I state the obvious. "Well, I'm not a normal person, am I? Remember, I'm the idiot who decided thirty minutes with you was something worth trying."

Spencer tosses an avocado into the fruit bowl. "Is this the cue to establish ground rules for you living here?"

"No. Because I will absolutely not walk around as if you are the commander of the house and I shall obey."

His brow raises, and I feel like a dirty thought just slipped into his brain.

"And here comes your stellar snark," he says, sarcastic.

I feel anger boiling. "You, likewise, have nothing nice to say about me. Can we just agree that we will stay out of one another's way? Which means when I am cooking, then leave me the hell alone."

"I believe you just set a rule which you were adamant we don't do." Smartass is really going all in on the irritation front.

My hands finds my hips, and I'm now just agitated. "We will only go in circles in every conversation. Shall we end this now before I throw something?"

"I'm a good catcher." He offers me a contrite grin.

I step closer to him. "You know, for someone who is a pitcher and throws curveballs, you sure as hell don't anticipate them. So, thank you, Spencer, thank you for ensuring we both end up in a situation like this where I have to be stuck under your roof because of your mistake."

He scoffs a sound. "Because your life was going so well." He walks past me, his shoulder hitting my own.

As he leaves the kitchen, I know his words hurt because insecurity is a bitch.

———

It's a little brisk, I'll admit that. The water in the lake, however, is doable for a quick swim. A fast swim is what it will need to be, as the sun is setting.

Every stroke is filled with my emotional state which could be a little calmer, I confess.

I hear Pickles' low bark. My faithful canine has been sitting on the dock watching me. I'm not quite sure he even knows how to swim or at least the water is probably too deep for him.

But I hear a splash, and I stop mid-stroke to assess the scene. Even treading water, I manage to roll my eyes when I see Spencer's sporty physique swimming in my direction.

I swim a few feet until I know my toes can touch the bottom, and Spencer meets me there.

After he walked out of the kitchen, I whipped up some cookie dough to set in the fridge and pulled together a chickpea salad. Keeping my hands busy in the kitchen was my distraction, just like Spencer going for a run or workout, whatever the hell star pitchers do in the off-season to keep themselves busy.

"You know this water is as cold as your heart," he informs me as he swims in place.

"Then why are you here? I would assume you have other

cool-off methods as part of your training." I move my arms to keep me afloat.

He shakes his head. "Because it's barely light out and you are swimming in a dark lake." His tone feels like he is scolding me.

"Not your problem."

"Really? Tell that to Hudson and Piper when we find your body in the morning." He takes me by surprise and grabs hold of me, bringing my body to his.

My breath catches in response. "Let go of me."

"No, we're getting out of the water, even if I have to carry you back."

I set my hands on his shoulders and that move catches him off guard. For a moment, we both stare at one another with the glow of the evening sky tracing our faces.

"I was almost done," I breathe out.

He doesn't respond instantly; instead, his eyes peer down and up. I know the temperature is causing two pebbles to appear through my suit. It's only when I study him that I realize that he jumped into the water still in his workout shirt and shorts.

"Don't you have strength training to do after your cardio? Clearly you are not following your schedule," I quip.

His hands swiftly move to my waist and in one go he lifts me into the air. "There. Strength training is done. Now can we get out of the fucking water, after you promise to keep your swims to the pool?"

He doesn't bring me back down, and I realize he is waiting for me to answer.

It is freezing, I can't deny it. I need to move as soon as possible. "Fine. I promise."

As if I am a delicate piece of glass, Spencer slowly brings

me back down into the water. Our eyes never part, especially when my body slithers against his.

"Good girl, now let's get the fuck out of here."

We both swim to the ladder on the dock and get out. I grab the towel that I had left earlier by Pickles and wrap it around my body.

Spencer is already walking away in a stormy mood. He jumped into the water unplanned, so he has no towel and his workout clothes are wet.

He seems angry, and I follow at a distance behind him. When he abruptly stops, I do too.

Spencer glances over his shoulder. "Do me one damn favor. You may hate being here, nor am I celebrating, but while you're here, try not to do anything that I wouldn't want a child to do. Lead by example."

My mouth gapes open. "Are you comparing me to a child again?"

His face looks pained, and he rubs his temples with his fingers. "That's not what I meant. I didn't mean…" He bites his lip and seems to be debating what to say. "All I'm saying is stick to the kitchen for getting out your stress, it's safer."

"I doubt that. Kitchen injuries have a lot higher statistic for emergency rooms than dark lakes."

Spencer rolls his eyes to the side, and I see a hint of a smirk because the outside lights in his backyard are on. A long breath escapes him. "Just get inside."

"I'll go inside because I want to go inside, not because you told me to," I say as I walk by him, well aware that I'm acting ridiculous.

"So cooperative," he retorts.

I don't look at him, but I can only imagine he follows me inside with annoyance as he probably should.

SITTING AT THE KITCHEN COUNTER, I tear a piece off a warm, gooey chocolate chip cookie and take a bite before I inspect the rest of the cookie. These are damn good.

I'm tired and should probably head to bed. I'm certainly not doing myself any favors by eating before bed, but I'm still taking in my surroundings and the fact that I am in this situation.

The man of the house enters the room, but I don't bother looking up from the plate of cookies. Nor do I care that I am in tiny shorts and an off-the-shoulder t-shirt. Might as well make myself at home.

"Vampires don't sleep, guess that explains why you're here."

I give him the death stare as he grabs a glass from the cupboard. "Nor does the devil, so I guess we know why you're not asleep."

Spencer leans against the counter. "That was some damn excellent salad. The chickpeas are exactly what I need for my protein intake."

My body straightens from the compliment; not many people have tried my new flare for cooking.

"Not too much lemon?" I narrow my eyes. He shakes his head. "Garlic balanced out?" He nods. "More feta next time?" His head bobs side to side.

Jesus, he is agreeing with me on all fronts.

"The poison should kick in soon."

He toasts his empty glass at me. "Wouldn't expect anything else."

I watch him pour a bottle of water into his glass before he swipes a cookie from the plate in front of me. A sound escapes his mouth that causes my eyes to widen slightly, a throwback to a time that shouldn't have been.

He enjoys cookies the same way he enjoys my pussy.

A long silence graces us, and I wiggle my fingers against the countertop.

"Do you have any hard liquor?" I shoot out.

"Are you sure that's a good idea?"

"After the way this week is going, yes, I'm sure. It's after 8pm, so I'm leading by example." I give him a cocky look.

He shakes his head ruefully. "All right."

Spencer walks to a high cupboard near the pantry and pulls out a bottle of tequila. I kind of assumed a guy like him would have a whole bar for entertaining, but alas, no.

A minute later, he has two shot glasses on the counter, and before he has a chance to find lime or salt, I pour a glass and quickly down it.

"Whoa, slow down, horsey." He takes the bottle from me.

"It's been one of those days," I lament and hold my glass out again.

"No shit. Want to talk about how you've been in a mood since the grocery store?"

Great, the reminder. I had nearly put the grocery store fiasco to the back of my head. Now that emotional boil begins to resurface… again.

"You have shitty timing," I inform him.

Spencer also takes a shot without the essential lime and salt. "I beg to differ. When it comes to baseball and sex, then my timing is right on par."

"Of course, you would say that. I just need no more surprises for a while.'

He pauses for a second and his jaw flexes side to side. "April, about the child comment—"

My hand flies up to stop him. "Don't remind me. You are

as bad as Jeff. It's not true, you know?" I hop off the stool and hold onto the shot glass for dear life. "I'm a fun person."

"Riveting," he deadpans.

But my rant continues. "I would have been a good wife. You know, sometimes two people just are not sexually compatible or maybe he is the one who's no good in bed. So good luck to his *new* fiancée. Besides, how wrong is he, I mean, I made a sex tape because I can be wild, so fuck him and his opinions," I ramble, take a shot, then realize to my horror what I just admitted.

My eyes shoot up to Spencer who is studying me intently. "Is that why he ended your engagement, because he thought you weren't good in bed?"

I avoid his eyes because this is beyond embarrassing. "Can we just ignore the last minute?"

"No, because it isn't true."

My gaze snaps in his direction, and I can't read his face. "You don't need to lie on my account."

The corner of his mouth hitches up. "When you talk, sometimes I want to ram a soap bar into your mouth, but damn, you have a talented mouth."

I feel my jaw drop because he has such strong conviction in his voice, and his words are probably the sweetest thing someone has said to me in a while, which has me questioning my sanity.

Spencer steps in my direction, and I feel like anticipation moves in a wave through me. I'm not sure what he's going to do, especially when his glass clinks against the counter when he sets it down in passing.

When he reaches me, his fingers grab my glass. "You may want to go easy with this." He sets it behind him on the counter.

"Show me the video."

He clucks the inside of his cheek. "Not a good idea."

"If you get to watch it then so do I."

"Why, because I was the point you needed to prove? The proof that you are not terrible in bed?" his voice rasps as he steps closer to me, invading my air. The heat of his body enters my realm. One step closer and we'll touch.

"Show me the video," I bite out.

"Admit my theory is correct," he counters.

I don't blink or move. My face feels tight but so do the internal walls between my legs. "Fine. You know my secret. What the hell was your excuse for that night?"

His lips stretch in a closed-mouth leer as the pad of his thumb finds my bottom lip. "Let it be known that I don't think this is the smartest of ideas. But okay, you are a player in our little show. If you want to watch the video, then we will do it right now."

I bite his thumb gently. "We?"

"My condition. I'll show you the video, but I get to watch you beg that night. So, would you like to keep it low-key and watch on my phone or should I connect it to the big screen?"

"Oh, now you know how to use technology," I snipe.

He chuckles, a sinful velvet sound, almost a warning.

"I need another shot for this," I admit because his conditions be damned. I'm going to watch that night on replay.

5

SPENCER

April sways her way to the sofa in the living room and sits on the edge of the cushions. Her facial expression is tight, but she splays her arm out to indicate the television.

Bold choice for screening options, but I like the enthusiasm.

"Again, I need to ask, as the mature one here. Are you sure you want to do this?" I ask and sit on the other end of the sofa. My thumb is already busy connecting my phone to the screen.

"Stop questioning it and just do it." April is a little on edge, but that only makes me grin because I am curious for her reaction.

I lean back against the back of the sofa and get comfortable. I hold the remote out in front of me ceremoniously.

"Here we go," I announce.

Glancing to my side, I see that April is playing with a strand of hair at the back of her neck, nervously twisting the gold lock around her finger.

Hitting play, I bite my bottom teeth into my upper lip

because it's not every day that this situation arises. And truthfully, I only watched thirty seconds, I haven't actually watched this in full.

My eyes focus on the screen. Conveniently my phone was on the desk dock which meant we got a frontal view of the bed where April and I stood in an argument.

I'm holding April by the waist as her hands grip my shirt. Admittedly, we are in an intense stare-off. Leaning in, I tangle my fingers into her hair. She doesn't flinch.

"You're despicable," she whispers.

"Good thing you hate me then," I murmur against her cheek as I pull her hair gently to bring her neck into a perfect angle for me.

"Insufferable."

"Feeling is mutual," I hum near her skin, a scent of sugar hitting me.

But then time stops, and I'm not sure who made the move, but our lips slammed together in a kiss. A hard, messy kiss that was equally energizing and addictive.

Different angles. Short gasps of breath. We seemed to be on a determined road to a destination that we were not quite sure of.

I watch the screen where April is tugging my shirt.

"See, I'm going to call that as you made the first move," I comment.

"Fuck off, Spencer, can we just watch this in silence?"

Looking at April, I see that she's pulled a cushion tightly into her lap, and she's looking intensely at the screen.

My eyes track a journey to the screen, back to April, and return to the movie where I'm pulling her dress down with no politeness.

"You have no respect for expensive clothing," she one-tone quips.

"Oh yeah? You have no idea how to work a buckle."

"This thing. It's a pain. Why won't it come off?" April says in a breathy tone as she looks down at her hands that are fumbling with my belt.

"April. It's a belt." I slow us down and give her knowing eyes as I show her how to unbuckle the basic accessory.

Her response is to push me back on the bed. "Asshole."

She's in a black bra and panties and is now straddling me, her pussy right on top of my cock. Using my arms, I walk myself up to sit, her breasts tight against my chest, and I reach my hands up to unclasp her bra, and when I kiss the curve of her shoulder, I notice my phone on the docking station on the desk.

"April," I say softly.

"Shh. Don't speak." She continues to attack my neck with her mouth.

I bring my hands to her shoulders to pause her. "Wait."

It gets her attention, and she looks at me as I peel myself away from under her, depositing her body to the side in the process like a toss of a ball into a glove.

"What the hell."

I walk to my phone. "Fuuuck."

"What now?"

"The video is on." I reach my thumb out to stop it.

"Don't!"

Creases form on my forehead as I look at her, my hand frozen in mid-air, and I feel an entertained smirk forming. "Don't? As in, let it keep recording?"

April is sitting on her knees, and I'd be lying if I said she didn't look cute as fuck with her tits pushed together between her arms at her sides.

"Now you're shy?" Her sass never fades.

"No. Just surprised you would want the proof for later that I've made you come more than once."

She snarls a sound. "Don't set yourself up for failure, sailor."

With that I give up on my phone and return to the bed in a flash, pin her down by her wrists above her head against the mattress, and urge her thighs open with my knee because I have a point to prove.

In the present, I feel April looking at me. It causes me to glance from the movie to April who immediately turns away when I catch her. She appears warm, or rather hot, and definitely bothered. Her legs are crossed rather tightly, and I have no qualms about admitting the fact that my cock is twitching against the fabric of my jeans.

"Want me to pause? Take in the fact that you were the adventurous one?" I haven't forgotten what she let slip earlier. It makes a little sense where her logic was that night and what a tool her ex was.

My guess is he couldn't deliver and placed the blame on April who is by no means a bore in the sack.

"No."

I slide along to couch closer to her, well aware that she is watching pre-season me licking her senseless with her body writhing under me while I had to use my hands to hold her hips down.

"Not an inch closer," she grits out.

"Why? I already notice that your hand is under the cushion. It's okay. Now isn't the time to be shy," I encourage her.

Her eyes dart in my direction. "Don't even suggest it." The movement of her chest bounces up and down, and the nipples under her shirt are hard. I don't see the outline of a bra which means there isn't one.

I unbutton my jeans and unzip. "Do what you want, but

I'm not going to stay constrained. Luckily, I'm king of this house and can do as I please."

April's jaw drops, but her eyes don't tear away from my hand that dips into my jeans.

"You really just want to watch? Your body isn't aching to be touched? Don't have a toy you packed?" I cast my doubt.

"Oh, trust me, it's more adequate than you."

I cluck my tongue. "I think the screen proves that theory wrong."

Quickly, she looks to the television where her fingers are threading in my hair as I lick her clit and bring two fingers inside of her. The volume is on low, but her moan is apparent.

Her eyes dart back to me, and she nibbles her bottom lip in contemplation before tossing the cushion to the side to make a point.

"You do your thing and I do mine, okay?" she breathes out.

She sinks her body into the sofa and her fingers disappear under her waistband, but her face is turned forward to watch.

On the screen she is about to come. I remember it well because she tasted like fucking strawberry shortcake, and as the sound in my living room confirms, she screamed my name and a flurry of F-bombs.

Making her come for some bizarre reason felt like a win, better than striking the batter out. I was determined to fuck her hard, and that meant making her come because I'm a team player.

I had only given her a few seconds to recover before I was pulling her by the arms up to sitting, and my ass is now in full view since she wrapped her mouth around my cock, as if she was eager.

Present me has my palm stroking my length, and April's

knee gently drapes near my own as she spreads her legs to get a better angle.

The camera position meant we only get to see the outline of April's hands holding my hips and her head bobbing. But I remember the way she took me as deep as she could go, and her tongue glided along my cock.

"That's a good girl," I praised her.

"You're right, if they only have this part of the video then it is all you, well, your ass, but mostly you," she comments, her voice breathy.

Looking to my side, I see that the loose fabric of her top has sunk low enough that I get a peek at her hard nipple. She is assessing me, and she knows what I want, which is why a sly smile curls on her mouth, and the fingers on her free hand find her nipple to play with.

"Your tits are always pert."

"Tsk-tsk, you should be watching the video."

"I think we both know that you took me to my edge before I slammed into your pussy with my cock where I made you come twice."

Her lips part open, and her arm with her hand in her shorts picks up speed, as does my own efforts on my cock.

We both glance to the screen where I had positioned myself over her, wrapped her legs around my waist, and worked my way inside her wet and tight walls until we both moaned in sync.

The next few minutes are a blur. A mixture of watching our present selves get off and our video selves move in different positions during sex. Video us were not delicate. April bounced on top of my cock as I thrusted up, I pumped inside of her with her leg over my shoulder as I kept her under me, and finally, we are on to the pièce de résistance, doggy style.

But I only watch snippets, as does she. Instead, our eyes are trapped in a locked gaze that our current selves somehow find sensual.

I want to slide my hand up her thigh to feel her, to soak my fingers in her readiness then bring her fingers to my mouth for a taste before she touches my cock.

But that's not our game right now.

Tonight is about watching.

The sounds from the television are only upping the ante.

In both timelines, we are almost there.

"You're going to come while watching me inside of you?" I husk.

"Uh-huh." She's in a daze of desire. Humans always act differently when an orgasm is at play.

The lids of her eyes hood closed, and my own pace runs hard.

An explosion of screen us and present us happens as we all come within seconds of one another, my heart rate fast as we come down, only for us to look at one another, and reality hits us like a ton of bricks.

WE SIT THERE in silence as the video comes to a stop. That night, she quickly dressed and told me to delete the video; in fact, she watched me delete the video and left.

Now we both try to straighten our clothes after watching our replay because I forgot my phone auto syncs to my cloud, or maybe deep down, I just ignored that piece of knowledge.

"See, we had good angles," I attempt to joke.

April's lips quirk out. "I mean, as far as performances go, then I think we hit it out of the park."

"I guess. I've never made a video, so can't compare."

Surprise fills her face. "Bullshit."

"No, really."

"Oh."

My shirt that I used to clean my stomach, I form it into a ball and throw it across the room in the direction of the laundry room.

The mood in my house has shifted, as you would assume happens when you decide to watch a sex tape that you made with a woman who costs a lot of energy, yet for some reason, I feel a slither of sympathy for her within me.

April abruptly stands. "We will never speak of this again."

Before I can even say, *"Here we go,"* she storms out.

There goes any prospect of having a discussion with her tonight.

Which is a shame because if she is going to stay here, then I need to share something else.

I blow out a breath because sometimes I still wonder how in the world I became a dad.

6

SPENCER

Leaning against my closed garage door with my hands in my pockets, I take a deep breath of the autumn morning air. I'm staring at the situation in front of me, the one that I should have had a few more days to prepare for.

My mother gets out of her car. Dana Crews is a force to be reckoned with. She may be pushing sixty, but make no mistake, she is in shape and is probably changing our schedule because she has a hair appointment to color the blonde hair that she's had for years.

"This isn't what we agreed." My voice is stern.

"Spence, this shouldn't even be up for discussion. The baseball season is over, and you know the deal," she chides as she circles around her car.

"The deal was until next week," I remind her. A deal is such an odd way to state our situation; there was never a negotiation, therefore it's more of a request.

She gives me a sympathetic look. "You are already missing so much; you should be relishing these moments."

She has a point, and it's what I want to feel, but this is a complicated situation.

"Besides, your father and I booked a last-minute weekend away and there is no school today for Teacher Institute Day." That's good, they deserve it.

My mom opens the back door of the car and immediately puts on a silly face for the passenger in the car. "Guess where we are?"

I walk a few steps so that I'm in view, and I do have a curiosity, even excitement somewhere within, however mostly I feel fear.

Maybe I soften an ounce when I see my six-year-old daughter give me a little half-smile. Her blondish-brown hair is up in a bun, and she is in a black leotard with pink tights and a tutu.

"Hey, Hadley." I give her a tiny wave.

Hadley's mom is no longer—or rather never was—in the picture, and my mom pretty much raises Hadley when it's baseball season. My parents have a house here in Lake Spark that I bought for them a few years ago so that there is no disruption to Hadley's school schedule. I've always been in Hadley's life in some way, but it feels like we are strangers to one another sometimes due to my schedule. It's a confusing time for her, I'm sure.

My mom helps my daughter out of the booster seat, and Hadley walks to me before she pokes my leg with her finger. "I'm staying with you now."

Awkwardly, I scratch the back of my head and lean down to her eye level. Her brown eyes are filled with curiosity. "Yeah, kiddo, you are. Remember what we talked about?"

"Yes. Sometimes I stay with Grammie and other times with you."

"Very good. You're going to stay with me for a while now, until spring."

"Right. Baseball." She seems deflated. I wish she was more excited about my career. Isn't it the dream? Saying your dad is a professional athlete?

I touch her shoulder. "But that's exciting, right? I mean, I have the pool, your playroom is all set up."

She nods her head and begins to walk in the direction of the door, dragging her feet.

I quickly go grab her bag from the trunk and grab my mom's attention in the process. "She doesn't want to be here."

"It's difficult for her too, but give it a day or two and she won't want to leave," my mom assures me.

Closing the trunk, I sigh. "I'm not here alone." I just get it out.

My mother's eyes grow wide and she looks elated. "You have a new girlfriend?"

"No. Just a…" I pause for a second, as I have to swallow around this lie. "Friend. Hudson's niece, actually."

Her brow raises. "Just? Hmm."

No, Mother, we made a sex tape, and the world may soon know.

"Really. She would rather see me on a BBQ skewer, but for a, uh, project it was easier if she stays here." I plaster on a fake smile. "I thought that I had a little more time before Hadley would be here."

We begin to walk side by side back to my house.

"She doesn't know about Hadley, I assume?"

"Not many people do, Mom, you know that. Besides, it's better that way because I enjoy my privacy. Anyways, April wasn't awake when I woke for my workout, and by the time you called to let me know you were two minutes away, unplanned, then I haven't had a chance to prepare her."

Holding the door open for my mother and balancing a bag in one arm, I lead us inside.

A pitched squeal fills the house, which fills my blood with a compelling need to run straight in the direction of Hadley's sound. Dropping the bag by the stairs, I run to the kitchen and into a scene that instantly makes my lips curl into a smile when I stand in my tracks.

April is wearing pineapple-print pajama pants and a tight tank top, and she's standing in the middle of the kitchen with a spatula in the air, a dusting of flour on her cheek, with her eyes glued on the little pink tutu in the air because Hadley is leaning over to pet Pickles, who is in the exact same spot as when I woke up and tried to convince him to go for a walk with me.

"You got me a puppy!" Hadley's excitement hits a new level that I didn't know was achievable.

And now I'm about to pop her dream. "Pickles belongs to April. He's staying here for a little bit."

"Oh." Hadley is disappointed but now sits on the floor and hugs the dog.

My eyes draw a line from my daughter to April who still hasn't moved, including the spatula in mid-air. "I have no idea what is happening," April admits one-toned in a daze.

I look at my mom, and my face must show that I'm struggling to come up with words. She affectionately touches my shoulder. "Maybe I should give you two a minute before I head out?"

Blowing out a long breath, I turn my focus to April.

"Who's April?" Hadley asks as she somehow managed to get Pickles to lie on his back with his paws in the air.

"A friend," I say.

"What's going on? In no world am I your friend," April mumbles, as she can't seem to tear her eyes away from Hadley.

My mother chuckles softly. "I like her."

"I'm Hadley. My daddy lives here," Hadley announces, and I'm not sure if it's from pride or because even for her age she isn't afraid to be bold.

April nearly chokes before her jaw drops, and her head makes a sharp turn in my direction.

"Can I see you for a minute?" I request nervously.

April quickly turns the stove off where she was making something that resembles pancakes and follows me down the hall to the laundry room.

The moment we step through the open doorway, her eyes bug out at me. "What the hell? Daughter? You don't have a daughter. There is nothing in this house to suggest that you, Spencer Crews, are a father, let alone to a little girl in a pink tutu."

I grab her arm. "Well, *April*. I *am* a father."

"This doesn't make sense. She just like, *poof,* magically appeared." April's hands make gestures to accompany her words. "Not one single clue in this house screams that you are rocking the dad bod," she reminds me again.

My eyes squinch together, and I nearly groan because I'm already tired of this conversation. Pulling her by the arm, I walk us across the hall to the other door.

"Why are you taking me to a closet?" April protests.

"It isn't a closet."

"Yes, it is—" I open the door for her, holding it open with purpose while she peeks her head in. "Oh." Her voice drops.

April takes in her surroundings, a room filled with toys. A playhouse in one corner, a wall with different levels of shelves filled with books and puzzles, a pink rug in the middle, and a dreamcatcher stenciled on the wall.

"Yeah, *oh*. Not my fault if you don't take in your surroundings."

April shoots me a glare. "Snooping around was going to happen today. I've not even been here 24 hours, and I got sidetracked yesterday for many reasons… as you know." Her tone is sharp, and her hip is tipped out. "Besides, it looks like a closet door."

"Doesn't matter. Hadley is here now and will be staying. I thought she was going to arrive next week."

"When were you going to tell me this important information?"

I rest my hands behind my head as I stretch. "When the moment was right."

April seems at a loss of words. "H-how come you never talk about her?"

"I'm protective."

"Still, at some point in the last few years of knowing you, then surely she would have come up in conversation." April seems to be in disbelief, and I get it. Hadley is my best-kept secret.

"Can I get into the details another time? Preferably when alcohol is involved?" Because the story isn't easy, nor what she probably assumes.

April nods her head in agreement. "Fine." She points her finger at me. "Any more surprises you have in store for me? Or are we done on that front?" She doesn't seem impressed, which is understandable since I keep throwing grenades at her lately.

"I'm not making any promises, because I don't know what I may need to do to keep you in line."

She scoffs a sound. "Cute."

She moves to walk away, but I instantly grab her arm to stop her. "Where are you going?"

"I'm going to meet up with Piper for coffee. I think it's better that I get out of the house for a little bit. You know what, maybe it's not such a great idea that I'm here. The whole sex tape thing will blow over, right? I mean, surely we're overreacting."

I give her a peculiar look as she rambles nervously. "Even more reason for you to stay. If it does leak, which it won't, but if it does, then the last thing I need is any more reason for it to turn negative. I have an image I need to maintain for my contract, and also for Hadley, who may look back one day at articles."

I swear a flare of empathy warms April's brown eyes before she swallows. "Okay."

She doesn't move, nor do I, and our eyes are locked in a moment that feels like we are even on the vulnerability front. I know the reason her fiancé left her, and she knows about Hadley.

And for some reason, even though I don't need to, I even the playing field even more. "That night," I begin.

April glances away then back to me.

I continue, "I needed an escape for one night."

A hint of a smirk tilts the corner of her mouth. "Must be something in the Lake Spark water then, because you chose to spend it with me," she attempts to make a joke.

We both acknowledge the realization of why that night happened. Our own personal reasons led to finding refuge in one another's arms, of someone we love to hate.

April makes a sound with her tongue, debating how to leave. "Uhm, I'll be back later. I think a breather for a second or two and coffee is a good idea."

"Sure." I step back with my hands in the air to give her

space before leaning against the wall with my arms folded over my chest.

She slowly walks away and then stops to look over her shoulder. "I kind of have a lot of questions about the whole you're-a-dad thing, like, *a lot*."

"Understandable."

She returns on her journey to the stairs but pauses again and turns to me with her finger in the air. "The apple sauce. It's for Hadley, isn't it?"

I nod in agreement.

"That's a relief. I've never known a grown man to eat from an apple sauce jar with a cartoon on it."

I scratch my cheek, trying to suppress my laugh.

"Super confused," she whispers, and I can tell she is still taking in the situation, but she continues to make her way upstairs.

I give myself a moment to consider the predicament that I find myself in. I have two girls living in my house. One a woman who speaks her mind, often at my expense, yet she just gave me a temporary truce for the last ten minutes. The other is a little girl who I wish would tell me the thoughts in her head. Now I have to balance them both in one house.

7
APRIL

I scoop out the jellybean from my coffee. I'm sitting in Jolly Joe's, the soda shop-styled candy store, ice cream parlor, and bakery that decided that putting jellybeans in coffee was a good idea, but it's truly revolting.

"Surely the bean melts in my coffee, so essentially my no-sugar latte is now a sugar latte." I highlight this fact to Piper who's sitting across from me bouncing her baby daughter in one arm and stirring her latte in the other, sporting her big shiny wedding ring on her finger.

Piper glances around the store, which is decorated like an old soda shop, including a jukebox in one corner. "It's fun. You never know what color you'll get," she points out.

Taking a sip of my, okay, admittedly delicious coffee, I hum an answer that maybe she is right. Setting my coffee down, though, I must point out the obvious. "I'm kind of done with the surprise train for a little bit."

"Why?" She scouts the room then leans in to whisper, "Sex tape wasn't enough for you?" Her humor causes me to roll my eyes because only she can get away with it since she's my best friend. "Is that freaking you out?"

"Nah. His lawyer is only the best, she works in my mother's firm. I mean, she hasn't lost a case in like forever. The sex tape is looking tame compared to other events. Apparently, Mr. Pain in my Ass—"

"But is he, though?" Her voice is full of doubt. "Sounds like you enjoyed the view of his ass at least once in your life." Now she's just teasing me.

However, the image of the video plays in my head. The part when he pinned my arms above my head against the mattress, and then a flicker of the scene from last night when his eyes landed on me as I watched. Heat runs through my body, but I shake it off.

My signature unimpressed look appears, which only makes Piper chuckle more. "Must we remind me of the error of my ways?"

Piper smiles. "I'm sorry. You're right. What else has Spencer done?"

"So, after imprisoning me in his house due to his lack of understanding for how his damn phone works, I get another surprise this morning."

"Ooh, mysterious. What could it be?" Piper looks at Gracie with a funny face.

I slide my coffee cup to the side. "Spencer is a father, apparently. A little girl just magically ran into the kitchen when I was attempting to make my crepes as a form of stress relief."

Piper's face turns serious, with her eyes darting in my direction, and clearly, she is studying me. Her lack of words makes it obvious.

"You knew?!"

Piper slowly nods.

"Why didn't you tell me?" I wonder.

Piper pulls Gracie close to soothe her by stroking her cute

little baby hair with her hand. "It's not my story to share. Besides, up until yesterday, I thought you and Spencer couldn't be within a foot of one another, so I assumed you would be the last person he would want to know."

I open my mouth but struggle to get words out until they fall off my tongue. "Now that explains why he looks like a pro at holding Gracie in the photo you sent in the family chat group."

Piper's brow raises, and I can see a smirk that wants to spread on her lips. "Oh, so you noticed that."

Sighing, I blow out a breath. "The man doesn't have many positives going for him, so the very minimal pluses are noticeable. I'm slightly confused, where is Hadley's mother in all of this?"

Piper's face turns saddened. "Not my story to tell," she reminds me.

My little cousin reaches her chubby little hand out for me. Piper offers Gracie to me, and I'm quick to shake my head no.

"You know I'm not great with kids."

"You are fine with kids," she corrects me.

My lips quirk out, and I lean into my hand on my propped elbow. "I guess I have no option, as my new roommate comes with a pint-sized girl in a tutu. Oh, crap!" I throw my hands into the air and quickly grab my phone from my jacket pocket.

"What now?"

I find Spencer's name in a chat conversation. "I was in such a shocked state that I quickly changed and left. I forgot Pickles. See? I can't even take care of my own dog!" I'm horrified, I never forget him.

ME

> Uhm, I think Pickles may need to go outside. Sorry, I forgot to bring him with me.

I drop my head into both my hands. I feel like a hot mess.

"Did something else happen? You seem a bit flustered or out of sorts."

I may have watched your neighbor come last night.

I look at Piper like she's crazy. "The last twenty-four hours have been a whirlwind. Oh my God, I didn't even mention about the general store yesterday. I was there stocking up on supplies when I ran into Jett."

"Jeff's brother?"

"Yeah, and he made sure to let me know that Jeff is now engaged, because clearly, he found someone suitable," I say, sarcastic.

Piper gives me a pained look. "Ouch. What did you say?"

I pause for a moment when I recall what happened. I slowly take a sip of coffee and set it back on the table. "Well, uh, Spencer might have, kind of... you know." I brush it off.

"I don't know," she states plainly.

"He made it look like we were there together. I guess so I don't look like a pathetic loser, you know."

A satisfied smirk appears on Piper's face again. "Really?" Oh gosh, it's one of those incredibly interested *reallys*.

"Can we stop talking about him?"

"You know, Hudson thinks you two would be kind of good together," Piper points out as she grabs a toy from her bag.

"Hudson is kind of positive about most things."

My phone pings a sound.

> **SPENCER**
>
> Figured. It's fine. He finally moved when Hadley went outside to play. He doesn't seem to run far, so I didn't bother with the leash.

The photo he attached unnerves me for some reason. Pickles is lying on the driveway with his head perked up. Thick chalk crayons are scattered around him, as he is next to Hadley who is drawing.

> Oh. Thanks.

I tap my long fingernail on the screen, as I'm just not used to this interaction with Spencer. It takes some getting used to.

"So, what's the plan for while you're hiding out in Lake Spark? Babysit your favorite baby?" She sounds hopeful.

"No. But I will accompany her if her mother is present." I smile sweetly.

Piper shuffles in her seat. "But seriously, what are you going to do?"

"Actually, the only bonus of this situation is that Spencer has an amazing kitchen, so I can practice all my recipes. Maybe I'll start that blog I keep talking about."

"That's a great idea!"

"Yeah, figured that I should probably start a new career chapter soon. My mother's daily texts are starting to sound concerned." I lean back in my chair.

Piper is now shaking a little rattle. "When I talked to Catherine last night, I played dumb and said the last I heard from you was that you had a date with some doctor, which got her a little excited."

"It really sucks my mom is your sister-in-law. I sometimes wonder if your loyalty has changed," I say, entertained.

"Nah, you have my full loyalty. I haven't even mentioned this situation to Hudson yet, but that is pure luck. I would never break news before a game. But after the game…" She rolls her eyes.

I wave her notion off. "He is the least of my worries."

"So, are you ready to head back *home*?" Piper flashes her eyes at me.

Looking into my empty cup of coffee, I growl a sound. "Guess I can't hide forever. Besides, I wanted to make pasta from scratch, and that's time consuming."

"I won't hear you screaming at Spencer from across the street?"

"No."

"Good. You never know what will happen."

"Nothing." I stand and grab my jacket from the back of the chair. I can tell Piper doesn't believe me, but we don't talk about it, as we are too busy getting Gracie bundled up and into her stroller. Piper is going to check on her boutique where she sells pajamas and lingerie.

Coincidentally, I was wearing her pajama design this morning when a little girl ran into my life and her father stood by, visibly ready to share another insight into his life with me.

———

Returning to Spencer's house, I immediately hear Spencer and Hadley when I walk through the door from the garage to the hall near the kitchen.

"I don't eat that!" Hadley sounds frustrated.

"Well, you have to, otherwise no apple sauce." He has an authoritarian tone.

"Grrr." Hadley actually just growled at Spencer like an animal, and it causes me to smile to myself.

I pass Pickles who is sleeping on a bed of blankets that I don't remember putting there. I lean down real quick to pat his head. Walking slowly into the kitchen, I see Hadley sitting at the kitchen counter and Spencer attempting to put a sandwich on her plate. All eyes turn to me.

"Hi," I hesitantly greet them and wave my fingers in the air for a little greeting.

Spencer sighs, and for the first time ever, I don't think I am the cause. He looks like he is exhausted.

"Hi." Spencer rubs his temples. "I guess you are owed a proper introduction. April, this is Hadley. Hadley, you remember April from this morning."

"Dog lady," Hadley announces.

Spencer chuckles. "I think you mean Pickles' owner?"

"Well, if Pickles likes me more, then maybe I can keep him."

I lean over on the other end of the counter, a good distance from everyone. "Let me guess. You made a bed for him?"

She nods her head.

My eyes slide to Spencer. "I guess I have competition." There is a moment's pause. "So, what's shaking?"

What's shaking? Yikes, I'm clueless how to communicate.

"Hadley isn't really a fan of food. She only eats apple sauce, donuts, and fries."

"Solid food groups," I comment.

He throws a kitchen towel to the side. "Yeah, I'm sure the pediatrician would agree." There is a lack of assurance in his voice.

I crawl my fingers on the counter as I debate what to say

or do. "Well, if you don't mind, I'm going to get to work on my pasta."

"Is that what I bought yesterday?" He indicates his head to the cardboard near the sink.

I walk straight to the box. "Yep. A pasta maker." I begin to work on the box.

"What's a pasta maker?" Hadley asks.

I focus on my task as I speak. "It helps me roll out the dough that I'm going to make."

"Is it messy?" she continues her line of questioning.

"Can be. I need to use a lot of flour."

"Can I help?"

My eyes immediately find Spencer who is avoiding my gaze. I look between them both, and I'm not sure no is really an option right now.

"Sure. But you might need to change. I would hate to ruin your ballet outfit."

"Getting her to change hasn't been a winning point today," he mutters.

Hadley bounces up in her chair. "Can I throw the flour?"

I laugh as I set up the machine. "Maybe not throw, but you can help me roll."

"Okay." She jumps off the stool and runs in the direction of the stairs. I make a mental note that I need to figure out which bedroom is hers. I'm going to assume it's the one near Spencer's that I thought was a door to a linen closet, because I seem to think Spencer has a gazillion closets.

A clearing throat draws my attention to Spencer.

"She isn't great with listening or eating," he states. "You also don't need to be afraid to say no."

"Duly noted."

Awkward silence floats between us, and I hate it. "Any news on the situation?"

He shakes his head. "No. An injunction was issued, and I have confidence in my lawyer. If she says not to worry, then I won't worry."

For some reason, I trust his words, and I should question that more.

"Who hacked you?"

"Probably the same guy who hacked a teammate and wants money. He might not even have the video and is waiting to see if we'll call his bluff. He sent us each a message, but I didn't answer, only had my team check it out. I'm not the first famous person to have this happen. I don't know more, but since it isn't just me then the lawyers actually have a better chance."

"Right." Why am I too calm about this? I should want to know every detail. Instead, I begin my quest around the kitchen for items that we got at the grocery store yesterday.

"Aren't you going to ask?" Apparently, Spencer notices my focus is on other topics.

I play it cool, but I am bursting at the seams. "Okay. What's the story with Hadley?" I grab a bowl from the shelf.

"She's mine." There is strong conviction in his voice.

"Got that when she announced you were her daddy."

"Our relationship is a struggle sometimes due to my career," he mentions, and it pulls a pin on the grenade inside of me that sometimes surfaces.

I set the bowl down with a bit of force because the bomb inside me just detonated. "Tell me that I'm not about to hear how you put your career first. I don't need to hear you one of those guys who just hands the kid off to the nanny." I scoff.

Spencer steps forward and grabs my arm, pulling me to him and taking my other arm too. "No. I'm. Not." He seems offended. "What the hell. You just want to think the worst of me."

I close my eyes, and I recognize my own insecurity and how I'm out of line. Opening my lids, I own up to my error. "I'm sorry. My biological dad isn't in the picture so lack of fathers is a touchy subject."

He loosens his grip on my arms. "Right. I forgot about that."

It's not a hidden fact that my mom used sperm donation so she could experience motherhood when she had nobody in her life because she was married to her career and felt she didn't have much time left on her clock.

"As much as I think it's great that I am the product of sperm donation and my mom was able to have me, because she is a great mom, I can't help but be slightly mad at Mr. Anonymous because he doesn't want to know who I am." It's the sore point of my life. Part of me is thankful that he gave the gift to my mom, otherwise I wouldn't exist. The other part of me simply can't comprehend why he wouldn't want to know who his child or children are.

"I get that. But it's not the same situation." Letting go of me, we don't take a step apart.

"What *is* the situation?"

"I've always been in her life," he states, and it feels like he has a point he wants to prove.

"Okay."

He walks to the fridge and grabs a beer. "Just trust me, I love her like a father should."

My breath catches because his words strike me in an unusual way. But before I can speak, the sound of feet running down the stairs draws our attention to Hadley in leggings and a t-shirt, closing the opportunity for more questions.

"Can I have an apron?" she requests as she runs to the

counter. It seems more of a demand that she throws at Spencer.

"You mean please?" he corrects her with eyes that feel like a warning.

I shake my head, accepting that the conversation Spencer and I just had needs to be replaced by focus on Hadley's entertainment.

Spencer looks to me as he begins his journey to where I would assume he hides aprons.

I try to take in the information that Spencer just told me, but questions are still popping up, and I don't have time to think because a little girl claps her hands together to get my attention.

"Why are you staying here?" she asks curiously as she investigates the items I set on the counter.

I debate how to answer because I'm beginning to wonder if the original reason is the most important factor anymore.

"Because…" I draw the word out, as I'm not sure how to answer. "Sometimes baseball players do something that requires their acquaintances to live in their house temporarily."

"What's an aquit, akee—"

"Acquaintance. Someone you know but who isn't close enough to be a friend."

"So, you're not our friend?" The little girl seems very confused.

I sigh, as explaining this to a child, I need to take the easy way out and lie. "I am a friend. And friends use friends' expensive kitchens to cook."

"How long are you staying?" she asks as I hand her a measuring cup.

"As long as it takes," Spencer announces as he holds out aprons for Hadley and me.

Grabbing my dark apron, I notice his eyes are piercing with a sort of stormy command that irritates me.

Because my treacherous body has excitement swirling somewhere within me.

8

SPENCER

Hadley looks at me with her head cocked to the side and a puzzled look. My eyes dart from her curiosity to the dining room table where April has set up a formal dining setting around one plate and a fancy decorated dish with the tortellini that she and Hadley made from scratch. There is even a fresh basil leaf thrown on for good measure.

"Is this how every meal is going to go?" I ask as I watch April standing on a chair to get a better photo of the plate of food.

"Yes. But you are assuming I'm cooking for you." She takes a shot then turns her head to me. "I'm trying to do something with my life, and while in prison, I might as well make opportunities arise."

"Highly doubt my state-of-the-art kitchen, indoor swimming pool, and lake views are considered a prison."

April smiles sweetly at my daughter and then a hint of poison joins her smile when her eyes meet mine. The problem is, every time she attempts to show her dislike for me, it only comes across as a playful game that I have no problem participating in.

"Silly me and my choice of words. This is, of course, a completely wonderful five-star unplanned vacation." I roll my eyes, as now she is just overdoing it. "Okay, enough photos, methinks. Shall we eat dinner?"

"Eww. I'm not eating that," Hadley protests.

April seems ready to stand off against my daughter. She hops off the chair and brings her hand to her hip before leaning down to Hadley's height. "Strange. You helped make it, and when you weren't looking, I even put in magic."

"Magic?" Hadley seems interested.

April nods her head. "Yep. It makes little girls grow and makes their fathers be compliant."

"Compli—" Hadley attempts to say.

My hand lands on my daughter's shoulder. "I'm curious about this magic. I thought April was only capable of witchcraft," I mumble through my teeth.

April walks to the kitchen counter and grabs Hadley's plate to show her a different version of the pasta than on the table. Hadley's version is simpler with no fancy stuff. Just tomato sauce and cheese.

"What's that?" Hadley investigates the plate.

"Magic pasta for girls who want to wake up tomorrow with special powers."

"She won't eat that," I tell April, because Hadley is a picky eater, and sometimes, I feel to defy me, she avoids eating what I suggest on purpose.

April takes a slow step, as if she is about to walk away. "Fine." She sighs. "I guess Pickles and I will enjoy our superpowers tomorrow morning alone. I think the magic I added was for making donuts tomorrow, or was it to get your daddy to take you wherever you want to go within a ten-mile radius,

I don't quite remember." She taps her finger on her chin in contemplation, and I feel an odd sensation as I watch April make an effort with my daughter.

"Anywhere?" Hadley is suddenly invested in the situation again.

April pivots to look back at Hadley. "I mean, I guess if you have like six bites then that will be enough for the magic to kick in."

"I'm six!"

"Exactly. So..." She offers the plate.

Hadley takes a step forward and then another step. "Three bites."

"Five bites."

Damn, these two are in negotiations with one another like it's habit.

"Fine." Hadley doesn't sound thrilled but hops up on a kitchen counter stool, and April smiles proudly as she places the plate in front of Hadley before handing her a fork.

We both watch as Hadley slowly takes a bite, and relief hits me that I don't need to battle it out for her to eat again today, April did it for me.

April's gaze and enlightenment from her win shifts to me and her smile fades slightly, possibly because I have a new look on my face of appreciation for how April is putting her distaste for me to the side to put my daughter first.

AFTER GETTING HADLEY TO BED, I walk into the kitchen to find April setting the last of the dishes in the dishwasher. To my surprise, she left me a full plate of food. We didn't get a chance to eat. After Hadley ate her token bites, I brought her upstairs to get ready for bed. Bedtime is the one thing where things seem to gel between Hadley and me. It just runs smoothly.

"Is this really safe to eat?" I have to ask, as I'm not sure why she is being kind to me.

She gives me a death stare. "Not that you deserve it, but yes."

I make a point of grabbing a fork and take a bite, fully expecting to spit it out, as I don't take April for a cook, but the moment the stuffed pasta hits my tastebuds, I'm taken to another world. Garlic, mushroom, and thyme hit my tongue in an explosion.

"Damn," I nearly moan.

April flashes her eyes in agreement as she throws the kitchen towel to the side.

"Good?" She seems proud.

"No way Hadley would eat this," I note.

"She didn't. I made a different version for her. Cheese, and I pureed carrot into the tomato sauce so she will never know she ate a carrot."

I slowly swallow as I study her and wonder why she put in the effort for my daughter, but all I come up with is, "Thank you."

She nods once, and we don't speak any more about it.

"I guess pasta goes against your protein shake regime, but I was never agreeable to your needs."

"Not exactly true," I quip, and the air nearly leaves the room when we both take in that I'm referencing our one night together.

Clearing her throat, April walks to the fridge to grab two bottles of beer. "Shall we finish your explanation of your life situation?"

I take another bite of food to give me an extra second or

two, but she's right. It's time to finish our conversation from earlier.

Taking the bottle of beer she offers, I grab the opener lying on the counter to pop the cap. "Where shall I start?" And what do I want to share with her?

"I'm not sure."

I wrap my lips around the bottle to take a decent sip of the beer, a specialty brew called Matchbox. "My mom has always helped raise Hadley, because Hadley's mom never wanted to be a mother."

April leans over the counter onto her arms and holds her bottle between her hands. "Who is she?"

"Just a hookup who signed away her parental rights the same week Hadley was born."

She offers me a sympathetic nod. "I would say I could never understand how someone could do that, but I get it. Not everyone wants to be a parent. Her loss, Hadley is a cute kid."

"I would say so," I breathe out. "And Hadley doesn't come to my baseball games, so she has never been around the media. That's more because she's too young to sit through a long game."

"Baseball games do drag," April confirms, and I flash her an unimpressed glare. "But people in Lake Spark know?"

"One of the joys of this small town is that everyone keeps what happens here in our bubble. I mean, your best friend and uncle literally walked around for months in Lake Spark together with not a word coming back to you."

"True." She rolls her eyes.

"And I've never brought Hadley to any of Hudson's parties since she's a young kid."

April straightens her posture. "That explains a lot. But I don't understand you."

"What do you mean?"

"Your effort is..."

I get defensive and stand up from the stool, my hands landing on the counter that I tower over. "What the hell does that mean?"

She shrugs her shoulders. "I just mean that, well, hell, I don't need to protect your cherished emotions, but damn, Spencer, let go a little around her."

"What the fuck?" I feel steam brewing between my ears. She has some damn nerve.

"Okay, hear me out." She holds her hands up to try and calm me down. "You keep her a big secret. I mean, you literally compartmentalize her life here into two rooms in this house. I don't even see any photos of you both anywhere around. And outside? I mean, get her a swing or something that says, 'this is your yard too.' Instead, you have a netted area to practice your pitching."

"She can play outside," I'm quick to justify.

"When she asks to bring toys outside. Why did she mention during pasta-making that a babysitter is coming next week?" She gives me a stern look.

I bite my inner cheek trying to suppress my rage. "Because I need the help."

"It's off-season," she counters.

I circle around the kitchen island to get closer to April, because this chick makes something inside of me want to throttle her, as I don't need her parenting views.

"I need someone to help around the house, and last time I checked, I'm missing the housewife."

April raises a finger. "Ah, so you need someone to help clean and do laundry. Not play with Hadley while you try to avoid her?"

"I'm not avoiding her. I'm doing my damn best, and I

don't appreciate you criticizing me after only a day here of seeing us together. Don't take your daddy issues out on me."

April's mouth drops open then slowly closes before she abruptly turns and leans against the counter to take a sip of her beer. "You're right. I just hate to see anyone miss opportunities with their parents."

Her statement is like a knife to the chest because I couldn't agree more, but I'm not going to highlight that.

"No. You just want to make me the bad guy," I correct her.

"It's easier that way," she says before pushing herself away from the counter and walking away, calling to Pickles in the process.

THE NEXT MORNING, I wake early, as I normally do, and work out in my at-home gym before making a protein shake. By the time it's eight, I find it unusual that Hadley hasn't woken up yet.

Heading up the stairs, I slow my steps when I hear murmurs of voices.

"You smell like candy," my daughter states.

"Why, thank you." April doesn't seem to mind that Hadley must have made her way to the guest room.

"Your skin is more beautiful than Grammie's, hers has lines."

April chortles. "That's because age plays a factor."

"You're the same age as my daddy?"

"A few years younger."

I approach the room to see the door is open, and as I take a step into the doorway, I can't seem to tear my eyes away from the sight of April with a white towel wrapped around her body and a towel on her head, while her hands are busy using a makeup brush. Damn, the towel is barely past her ass, and I'm far too curious if she is still completely naked under it.

Hadley is leaning against the dresser in her pajamas, watching April.

Clearing my throat, I knock on the door pane. "Morning." I find my voice despite the image in front of me doing a number on my brain.

April doesn't take notice of me and focuses on the mirror. "Someone found me this morning."

"Sorry. I guess working on manners when a guest is here is new."

"Hey! It's more fun to watch April get pretty than go downstairs."

"Why is that?"

Hadley shrugs. "I don't know. She has sparkly powder."

"Sparkly powder? I think you are still stuck in your dreams, kiddo." I cross my arms over my chest.

April smiles. "Nah, she's right. I have this sparkly body powder that I was putting on when she came in."

My fist finds my mouth as I look away, and I'm now imagining where the hell that powder goes.

"Daddy, I don't think it's polite for you to be here. This is girls only."

I tip my head in the direction of Pickles who is lying lazily at the edge of the bed. "Pickles is here."

"He doesn't count," Hadley justifies.

"She's right, you know," April pipes up. "Your eyes should be somewhere else other than the room where I slept all night, only to wake, shower, and am now wearing a towel that could fall at any moment." I hear her taunting me as she applies mascara.

"See? You need to leave," Hadley declares, completely unaware of April's innuendo.

I shake my head ruefully. "Fine. But you are coming with me, Hadley, you need to get ready for the day."

Hadley's finger finds the air. "Did the magic work? Since I ate my bites of food last night. Do we get to go anywhere I want?"

I open my mouth, but then hesitate, remembering what April said last night about making an effort with Hadley. "Sure. Jolly Joe's?"

"Uhm, I want to go to Pioneer Park."

"That's still around?" April wonders. "I used to go there as a kid."

Fuck. It's Saturday, which means Pioneer Park will be packed with little heathens that I can't stand. I only like select children who tend to have parents whom I know.

"Can we?" Hadley brings her hands together as she pleads and bounces in her spot.

"Oh, sounds fun," April says, taking pleasure in this. "Merry-go-rounds, weekend parking, kids, people, autographs, farm animals, more people, all the things your daddy loves."

A sly smile spreads on my mouth. "Sure. Pioneer Park it is, *and* a special guest of honor will join us."

"Really? Who?" Hadley's face lights up.

"Princess Sparkly Powder herself," I declare.

It grabs April's attention, and she turns to face me with a tight smile. "I'm joining in?"

"For crowds, candied apples, more kids, and people in costumes? Not to mention proof that I'm an attentive parent. *Absolutely*." I don't blink, as April and I are in a locked gaze.

April takes a deep breath. "Fine. But we are stopping at Jolly Joe's for my coffee, so sign me up for this adventure."

Hadley is already running off, listing what she will wear, leaving me in her wake to look at the woman who wants to challenge me on everything.

"Might want to wear a sweater. It might get nippy out, and we know how your nipples get," I suggest with a satisfied smirk.

She begins to untie the knot of her towel above her perky tits. "Sure. I'll just get naked first. Are you going to turn around or pull out your phone that you don't know how to use?"

April turns around, dropping the towel to reveal a very naked back and a black thong. She takes pleasure in teasing me because that's what it is. There is nothing about the last five seconds that I hate.

She is a willing participant in the image that will now haunt me all day for our impromptu group outing.

9
SPENCER

My head lolls to the side against the driver's seat headrest. I blow out an exhausted breath as April gives me a knowing look.

"What? Your beast of a car could totally fit in that spot back there."

I look at her like she's crazy. "No way, I can't risk scratches, and this isn't a beast. This is the latest model of the best SUV on the market because I have precious goods to drive around."

We've been circling the parking lot of Pioneer Park for only a few minutes, and April wants to comment on my driving at every chance.

"Fine. Looks like we just have to get in line after that birthday party group that just arrived in a big van." She tips her head forward slightly to the car up ahead.

Ugh, more people, just thrilling. I steer the wheel to an upcoming spot that is far too small for my liking. I don't even need to look at April while I park to know she has an accomplished smirk on her face.

"Yay, we're here." Hadley is already reaching for her seatbelt.

"Just easy when getting out. Let April help you," I call out over my shoulder.

The next minute, we're working our way out of the car, meticulously holding doors and squeezing through tight spaces before we commence our short walk to the ticket counter—or the gates of hell as I like to call it.

Pioneer Park isn't quite a major theme park, but it's a step up from the typical park-district petting zoo. There is a little train you can ride on, a classic merry-go-round, a mini old-fashioned town, animals, and people dressed as pioneers.

Standing in line for the entry tickets, I hear tiny voices chattering, and before I can investigate, April is nudging my arm. I swipe my sunglasses off my face to get a view.

"Aren't you going to wave hello to your little fans?" April gives me a scolding look.

Looking over my shoulder, I see a few boys maybe a year or two older than Hadley staring at me with amazement.

Giving April a serious look, I tell her point blank, "No."

"Grumpy," she mumbles.

"I'm not grumpy. I'm trying to have a weekend with Hadley." We step forward as the line moves.

"And they are kids. Isn't gratitude one of Hadley's theme words at school this week?" She is completely making that up, but it's effective.

Hissing out my breath, I turn back to the boys and offer a short yet effective wave. The boys instantly grin with excitement before their parents usher them along in the line.

A slow clapping sound hits my ears, and I turn to see April clearly congratulating my efforts. She's exasperating, but at least her efforts to annoy me are amusing sometimes.

"Daddy, I want to go straight to the log cabin," Hadley

says, pulling my arm.

"You're the boss."

After getting our tickets, we enter the fictitious prairie town, a sort of tribute to the area from years far back.

Hadley is already walking in the direction of where we need to go, and I can't help but notice someone else in our group moving with gusto.

"Someone is excited about the log cabin. When was the last time you were here?"

April glances to her side as we walk. "Years ago, but something tells me it hasn't changed. I wanted to go a while back for fun, but Je—, I mean, someone thought it was childish, so didn't want to play along. Besides, can't you smell the wood burning? I love it."

Taking a sniff of the air, I do smell the fire.

"I wonder if I can make a candle like last time," Hadley mentions before interlinking her arm with April's.

Watching them skip a few steps ahead of me, I don't like it. Hadley is taking to April, and maybe I wanted Hadley and me to be a team on our tolerance level of April. But now I'm truly two against one, and I can't help but feel an odd spark inside me that maybe all along I wanted April and Hadley to instantly click.

I do my best to ignore my mind meandering into unknown territory, but I seem to zone out slightly as Hadley and April approach the log cabin with excitement. A woman who looks maybe twenty is dressed up and is stirring a caldron over a fire.

"Something about 1800s-inspired fires just hit the spot." April takes in a deep inhale, stretching her arms into the sky as she stands next to me and watches Hadley disappear inside the cabin.

"Oh yeah, calms me completely," I say, sarcastic, as I

scan the scene to see that everyone seems to be in their own world.

Hadley waves through an open window, and I return the gesture.

"You know she is completely checking you out," April points out.

"Who?"

"Witch lady."

"I don't think she's a witch; did you not get the memo that pioneer times is the theme?"

April snickers and gives me a knowing grin. "Fine. The twenty-year-old who likes to dress up is checking you out while she stirs the pretend soup."

I glance at the woman by the fire, and she is shooting me some serious flirty eyes before her hands adjust her costume in a not-so-subtle way to boost her cleavage up. Crossing my arms over my chest, a wide grin spreads on my face when I turn to look at April who almost has a soft pout.

"Unlucky for her, I don't pick up women when I'm in Hadley's presence."

"Sounds more like her lucky day then." April tries to avoid her eyes, meeting my own. "Oh, look at that, the sheriff arrived on a horse, probably to arrest the soup-making pioneer for her scandalous ways." April is quick to power-walk to the scene to meet Hadley who is curious about the arrival of the character.

I can't help but smile at the fact that, if I do say, Miss April is a little jealous.

ENDING the call on my cell phone, I jog to meet up with April and Hadley up ahead. April hands me back my drink without ever losing focus on the brochure she and Hadley are looking at.

We're walking along the overdone Main Street of Pioneer Village, taking sips from our soft drinks.

April points to the upcoming old-fashioned post office on the right. "There. That's where I think bonnet-making is at one." She continues to look at the little brochure to double-check something. "After that, we can do the train."

"I think then we have pretty much seen everything," I affirm to our little crowd.

"Don't be such a spoil," April throws me some shade.

"That's one of our words," Hadley proudly reminds us.

Hadley and April have been going over the pioneer dictionary in the back of the brochure.

"It is. Now go *mosey* along so you get a good spot for bonnet-making." She scoots my daughter in the direction of the post office door.

April and I both slow our pace as we watch Hadley join all the other little girls sitting around a table.

"Huh. This word is fitting. 'Dander; a strong emotion or anger.' That's going to be my word of the day," April comments as she reads the paper.

Grabbing the brochure from her pink-polished nails, I skim the list. "Funny. I thought you would pick *hankering* as your word."

"Hankering?" Her eyes grow wide with intrigue.

"Yeah. In modern times, we call it desire."

Her mouth parts open and an undescribed sound escapes her mouth. "Trust me, that's not what I'm feeling today. I'm kind of wishing a plague or something was part of the theme here to wipe me out."

I click the inside of my cheek. "You're having a blast here. I can see it."

She studies me for a second before a smile erupts. "Okay, smartass, you may be right just this once." She playfully hits my arm.

"Was it the merry-go-round or riding the covered wagon that took you over the edge to happiness?"

"Both. I don't know, it's kind of nice being a kid again. What about you, grumpy? You don't seem miserable."

I debate if I should let a comeback fly off my tongue or be honest, and when I look at April's deep eyes as she wipes a strand of hair away from her face, I have my answer. "Hadley's happy, so I'm happy… and thank you."

"For what?"

"You're making this a nice day for her."

Her shoulders come up toward her ears, and she seems to brush off my compliment.

"She's a sweet kid; must have gotten that from her grandparents."

We both look at Hadley who is busy with crafts.

"She is. Just an unusual situation," I admit.

April taps my arm with hers. "Nah, many kids have only one parent and turn out amazing. Just look at me. And an unusual situation would be dragging your video partner along after making her stay at your house—oh, wait." She brings her hand to her mouth in pretend shock. "That's us."

The corner of my mouth tugs up from her humor.

I step into her space with my hand finding a spot on her lower back. "Watch it, April, I might have to throw you over my shoulder when we get back to the homestead." There is far too much swelter in my voice than I would care to admit.

Yet April just chuckles a sensual sound under her breath.

"Careful. I might actually tolerate you today," she warns.

And hot damn, I hate that I'm enjoying this flirtation between us.

10

SPENCER

By the time I'm driving up to my house, Hadley is out like a light. My neighbor Ford is busy unpacking his car. I wave at him as we pass. We're good friends too, and when we're both in the city for our teams, then we often meet up.

"Ford Spears is looking mighty fine." April looks on with wide eyes, but I get a sense that she is trying to rile me.

I sit a little taller in my seat. "Doubt it."

"Huh, I knew that his house was finally ready to live in, and he apparently now lives there, but he looks a lot hotter in person than what you see online."

Ford plays hockey and spent a lot of his childhood in Lake Spark too. Being in his late twenties and with his short haircut and trim physique, it gets a lot of attention from girls, apparently April included.

"Down, girl, I'm confident he is waiting for someone."

"Jealous?" She looks at me, amused.

"No... Hey, doesn't Pickles need a walk?" I change topics as I pull us up in the driveway.

"Yeah, he does. Should I wake Hadley?"

Parking the car in the garage, I turn the engine off. "Nah, it's okay, I'll do it. She needs to wake up or she won't sleep later."

A minute later, I'm peeling Hadley slowly off the backseat and into my arms, resting her head against my shoulder. I'll wake her once we're inside and I set her on the couch.

I notice that April is staring at me, her eyes fixed on the scene.

"You okay?" I whisper. "You look like your cold heart might actually be thawing."

Her lips quirk out. "Just noticing that… it doesn't matter." She twirls around and heads out of the garage before I can figure out what is crossing her mind.

I don't spend time trying to figure out where April's head is at, because I have my little girl wrapped in my arms. I have no illusions, I know that this won't last forever; Hadley is growing at record speed.

When I lay Hadley on the sofa in the living room and she begins to grumble as I slowly wake her, I feel like she is at a stage of life when I'm enemy number one. The teenage years already spook me, and we're not even halfway there yet.

"Come on, sweet pea, time to wake up." I tuck her hair behind her ear, but her little hand swats me away.

"Grr."

Her sounds only make me smile to myself because she is adorable.

"It's not even dinner time yet."

She slowly pulls herself up to sitting and rubs her eyes. "Can I watch a movie?"

"That's all you want to do," I note.

"Because you're not good at playing with dolls or drawing."

Hadley isn't afraid to speak her mind, sometimes ruthless,

but I can't even be mad. She has a point, I'm not great with playing, and I feel relief every time a babysitter comes to help out and play with Hadley.

"We can go outside to play. Want to throw the ball around?" I suggest.

"No. It's always me watching you practice throws."

"I can go gentle, grab the tee-ball set." I hear the eagerness in my voice.

She shakes her head in disagreement. "I don't like baseball, I like ballet."

I really struggle to find a mutual interest to bring us together. I'm the hard-ass who keeps my head in the game, and I don't have it in me to play dress-up or dolls.

"You had fun today, right?" I hear that I'm concerned on all fronts today. "I thought you wanted to go to Pioneer Park."

"I did have fun. April helped me find all the good places and pull you along." Hadley shuffles on the sofa to dangle her feet off the edge.

I scratch the back of my head. "Right. April."

"She's a fun friend."

"That she is." Damn it, she's outshining me. Maybe April staying here is a bad idea. I should be focusing on my relationship with Hadley, not adding extra roadblocks.

Hadley surprises me when she cuddles against my arm. "Don't worry. You're still really good at reading me stories, and you have connections to the tooth fairy, you promised you did."

A warm smile hits me as I loop an arm around her little body to bring her closer to me.

"I do have connections," I promise, because I know that phase is coming soon. Grabbing the remote from the side, I put on the screen to the streaming service. "Let me guess, Encanto?"

"Uh-huh."

Pressing play, I soak up this moment with Hadley, reminding myself that I'm trying.

The sound of dishes moving in the kitchen causes me to glance behind me to see that April must have been listening or watching, although she's pretending to focus on whatever she is creating.

A while later, with Hadley well into the movie and my tolerance for songs at a peak, I leave her with a blanket and head to the kitchen that is now empty.

Grabbing a water, I station myself at the kitchen counter and begin to skim my tablet, heading to the online toy store.

I tap my finger on the screen as I debate what in the world I could buy that maybe Hadley and I could both enjoy.

The smell of sugar hits me, and the feeling of another person walking behind me fills my body with a full feeling.

April walks straight to the oven to open the door and check on something, not saying anything to me in the process. When she seems to approve of whatever is cooking in the oven, she looks up at me and throws an oven glove to the side.

"Everything okay?" She rolls her lips in.

"Yeah, just looking at toys."

"I meant you escaped Encanto. Is it because you got to the scene about the abuela?"

"No," I say, defensive.

Her eyes narrow in on me "Really? Because I heard a rumor that you get emotional during that scene."

"Absolutely not." Or yes.

"Alright, I'll let it go, but I know your secret." She laughs. "And toys? You don't need more toys, you have plenty of those."

"I know, but something I could do with Hadley." I look

into the other room then back at my tablet. "What about Princess Legos?"

April offers me a soft smile. "I really think she has enough toys in her special room."

I begin my search in the bar of the website, but then excitement takes over me. "Maybe I should have someone install a ballet barre in her playroom."

"Now that is a perfect idea. She will go crazy," April assures me.

Something else dawns on me, a memory. "Aren't you the ballet pro?"

Our eyes catch because she knows I'm referencing that night.

"You twirl and bend like one, anyhow," I add.

She raises her brow but says nothing. I notice her cheeks blush a shade of pink. I pause for a beat and look at April who is watching me intently. "What's cooking?"

She blinks a few times. "Oh, that. Uhm, just a macaroni cheese bake, and truffle potatoes with chicken for the adults. Didn't have it in me to make stew or anything pioneer themed."

"It sounds good. What time is dinner?"

"Should be in twenty minutes, but I'm going to leave you two at it. I'm going to work on some things on my laptop." She seems to want to avoid us, and for some reason, that disappoints me.

April ignores us for the rest of the night, and it causes me to toss and turn when I should be sleeping.

W%%HEN I WAKE%%, I seem to run harder for my morning workout, as if something is bothering me, which makes sense considering my current life predicament. Standing on my dock on the lake after my brutal run, I pick up a baseball from the basket of many and throw it out across into the lake. I do this on repeat to relieve stress.

"Whoa, isn't this a waste of baseballs?" I hear Ford approach me, as he must have been on a morning run.

He jogs in place once he reaches my spot.

"Sorry. It's been a hell of a week." I stretch my arms over my head then throw another ball. "This is no different from golfers and their golf balls."

"Fair point. Nothing to do with the woman who was in your car yesterday? She looked familiar."

"April?"

"As in Hudson's niece?" He brings his foot up behind him to stretch his quad.

"Yeah, she's staying with me for a little bit."

He makes a winding gesture with his hand. "Hold up. You clearly haven't told your best friend what the hell is going on."

"She's the one." He looks at me, as if I need to offer up another clue. "As in the one from the wild night I had after Hudson's and Piper's baby shower."

Ford laughs deep. "Oh man, does Hudson know?"

I shake my head. "Trust me, it was one night only."

"Then why the fuck is she living in your house?"

"A complication arose."

His eyes grow big. "Like a nine-month-later complication?"

"No. As in 'we kind of did something and need to ensure nobody sees it' complication."

Ford now laughs hysterically.

"It's not funny."

"Yes, it is. Everyone knows that with a good lawyer you'll

be fine. I mean, how many guys on my team have done something stupid and nobody ever found out? It is way too many to count."

Raking a hand through my hair, I know he's right. "Anyhow, it's a temporary stay, and we argue most of the time."

"I do remember you mentioning you're not a fan. But why did you invite her to stay? You never let women near Hadley."

"I didn't have much choice. Besides, I can get away with saying she is a friend to Hadley since she's always around Piper and Hudson."

Ford bobs his head from side to side. "Maybe."

"Maybe what?"

He touches my upper arm. "You'll figure it out. I need to run, get my shake, and head back to the city." He begins to run in place.

"Don't forget about the charity dinner later this week," he says as he runs backwards. "You are expected not to come alone," he calls out.

I wave him off in the air with a little two-finger salute.

I take my time with a cool-off walk back to the house, making a mental note that I only left the house because I knew April was there in case Handley woke, which clearly happened as I hear them in the playroom as I walk past the hall. I backtrack a step but stay hidden as I listen.

"So, what should a princess expect?" Hadley wonders. They're sitting in her little tent with books scattered around on the floor. My daughter is still in her pajamas, whereas April is ready for the day in jeans and an off-the-shoulder sweater while she strokes Pickles' head.

"That her prince decorates the room with candles and makes it a special evening when he asks her for her hand in marriage. Most definitely not in their apartment while they wait for a taxi to pick them up and he suggests they get married." I can hear the truth in her voice. Honestly, it kind of sounds like Jeff's proposal, well… sucked.

"Hmm. Should there be cake?"

"Maybe. The prince should go all out on grand gestures."

"Can the princess be happy without both parents at her wedding?"

April's shock at the question is apparent in her pause. "Why, of course. What makes you ask that?"

"Because I only have a daddy."

"And? I only have a mommy; well, she found her prince recently, but he isn't my dad. Anyways, I still have every plan to be happy on my wedding day."

"Why don't you have a dad?"

"I was specially chosen by my mom. Sometimes we only have one parent, and that just means they have more love to share. I'll let you in on a little secret." I can hear her pretending to whisper. "They normally give us extra cookies because they want us to be happy."

I laugh softly, before I clear my throat and make my presence known.

They both look up at me.

"There you two are."

"He's up." Hadley doesn't sound thrilled.

April swipes Hadley's ponytail to the side. "Yes, because your daddy works extra hard to stay in shape to make millions of dollars off of throwing balls so he can buy you all the cookies in the world to show his love."

Why do I feel like a melting puddle of goo? And why does it not filter through my brain when I tell April, "Throwing a curveball at April makes my day complete, which is why you're coming with me to this charity dinner later this week… as my plus-one."

11
APRIL

What nerve that man has. I chop my peppers with extra vigor, slight aggression escaping me on every knife cut.

He actually thinks he can just order me to attend some charity event with him. He didn't even ask, just demanded. I don't even have anything to wear. I mean, I didn't exactly add black-tie attire to my suitcase for this last-minute trip. I stuck to a wardrobe appropriate for sweater weather, jeans and layers of shirts.

My phone vibrates on the counter, and I see my mother is calling. Blowing out a relaxing breath, I prepare myself for this and tap the green button.

"April, finally! I feel like you've been avoiding me the last few days." My mom seems to be sitting behind her at-home desk, with her blondish-brown hair tied in a low shoulder-length ponytail.

"Sorry." I lean against my propped elbow. "I've been busy with a project."

"Clearly. Where are you? That doesn't look like your place."

"It's not. I'm at Spencer's house."

"Spencer? As in Spencer Crews? Your uncle's neighbor? Star baseball player?"

I nod my head with dread for the upcoming minutes ahead of me.

"Why on earth would you be there?"

As much as I would say my mother and I are close, I'm not about to spill the beans on the true reasoning of how I ended up in the amazing kitchen with an asshole fastballer, who is currently playing outside with an adorable child.

"Uhm, he needed… a sitter." I doubt my lie that just came out then realize I shared a fact. "Can we throw in your lawyer confidentiality card for the last part? He doesn't really want people to know about his daughter."

My mother purses her lips together, and her expression is unreadable. "Sure," she simply replies. "But I didn't realize being a nanny was what you wanted career-wise."

"Oh, it's not. This is temporary. However, I do get to use this kitchen, and I've been nailing a few recipes."

A warm smile spreads on her face. "I saw. Your social media has some lovely photos and recipes."

"Anyway, when are you coming to Lake Spark?"

"To see my precious little niece Gracie?" she nearly coos.

I give her a fake unimpressed look. "I get it, the baby wins. Kind of hoped your badass adult daughter would get a higher ranking."

My mother chortles a laugh. "You're right. I'm happy to see you're okay. I had an odd feeling that something was up. Mother's instinct."

The corner of my mouth curves up. "And father's instinct. You have it all."

"I have no other choice."

"Do you think it goes the same way for fathers who raise

their kids alone? I mean, do they also have a mother's instinct?"

She shrugs her shoulders. "I don't know. Everyone parents differently, and families come in different shapes."

"That I know. It's just kind of weird seeing Spencer do the single-dad thing; it's so different to when you did the single-parent thing with me."

My mother folds her arms over her chest. "Well, I think it must be hard when he travels so much for baseball, but all that matters is that the effort is there. Sometimes as parents we put in a lot of effort, but things still don't happen the way we want it to. What's important is that we can never doubt we tried."

I'm not sure what to say, or why I asked. But then I recall the last few days and how my view of Spencer has been thrown for a loop.

The man watches braiding videos while he tries to twist Hadley's hair, he attempts to feed her vegetables when he knows no kid that age will agree, and he still takes her to places that make her happy, even when she gives him the cold shoulder.

"I think I might have been a bitch," I admit out loud.

My mom gives me a stern eye. "Elaborate."

"I might have been a little hard on Spencer."

Disapproval spreads across my mother's face. "April."

Geez, still she has the power to say my name to shake me into fear of a timeout.

My palm flies up. "Okay, I will be a little nicer… when it comes to Hadley."

"Good. You are full of kindness."

"He brings out the evil in me."

Her grin is a knowing one. "Hmm."

"Anyway, I need to get these stuffed peppers in the oven."

I begin to move, bringing my phone with me. "Wait. You knew about Spencer's daughter?" It dawns on me that Spencer is using her colleague to deal with our little situation, probably because he already uses their firm for all his legal woes. "Let me guess, he has used your services for family law?"

"I'm not at liberty to say."

That's a yes. I groan softly. "You don't talk about cases with Celeste by any chance, do you?"

"No. Not unless she needs my advice but won't mention names. Why? She asked how you were doing the other day, by the way."

"I'm just splendid," I deadpan.

"I'm sure you are." My mother sounds amused. "Bye, sweetie."

"Bye."

Kneeling down to look at the oven, I see the light is off to indicate it's warm and ready to insert my tray bake. My mind repeats my new rule that I will be nice to Spencer when it relates to Hadley, but for everything else, all bets are off.

———

I FOUND HIM.

After avoiding him all day, I arrive at the last destination where I can think to look for Spencer, and coincidentally, it's where I was going to head for the evening anyhow.

He's swimming his laps in the warm indoor pool, and the lighting is dim yet perfectly outlines his chiseled form. The light in the water causes a blue glow in the center of the room, and a wall of glass overlooks the lake.

Since this morning's demand, I've stayed out of Spencer and Hadley's way. I didn't want my anger to boil over in front of the little one, and I also thought maybe they needed some alone time since it's the weekend and tomorrow she is back to school. I went to the grocery store, walked Pickles, cooked, and left food for both of them while I went to check on Piper next door. As soon as I knew Hadley would be asleep, I began my quest to find the man.

Now I'm staring at Spencer, oblivious to me, as he creates waves in the pool from his long, deep strokes.

I whip my robe off and walk down the steps into the pool, wearing my deep purple triangle bikini that barely covers my globes, but cleavage is a girl's best friend.

Spencer must notice that he is no longer alone, as he suddenly stops and stands in the pool, shaking his head and wiping the water from his face.

"Ah, the mermaid appears, actually swimming in a pool this time."

"Well, I mean, this will do," I say as I submerge myself into the warm as bath water.

"I could have sworn you've been keeping to yourself all day on purpose, yet here you are in my pool." He walks closer to me, and now I have a full view of his bare chest and the tattoo.

"The number. It's her birthday, isn't it?" I comment. The anchor I know is a logo from the first team he played baseball on, but the number...

He looks down at his chest. "Could be. Days and months do have numbers."

Fuck, something just tugged on my heartstrings.

"I'm sorry," I blurt out.

"For what?" He looks at me, intrigued, and slowly moves closer.

"I was maybe a little judgmental of you in regard to Hadley."

His eyes nearly bug out. "No shit. Is this an apology, April?"

"Yes." I do my best to avoid looking into his eyes. "I know you try with her. And it can't be easy."

He takes in a breath, his nostrils flaring slightly. "Apology accepted."

I do a double take. Why is he being so agreeable? I thought he would make me grovel. We look at one another in amazement that we both just made it easy for each other. But then I remember that it was only part of the reason that I wanted to find him.

Immediately, I push against his hard pecs, causing water to swoosh around us. "You're unbelievable."

"Way to ruin a moment of peace. What the hell now?"

"You can't just order me around and tell me that I'm going with you to some charity event as your plus-one." I splash water at him.

He instantly pulls me close and turns us so I'm trapped between the edge of the pool and his body, his hands landing on each side of me, creating a wall.

"Oh, I can. While you're staying here, I need you to be on my team. We both have a lot at stake, and the more clues we leave, then the better it looks just in case the world sees how you scream my name." His tone has a sort of dominance that is irritatingly sexy.

I give him a pointed look. "And where are we with that? Any updates? I feel like this should be progressing so my ticket out of here is sooner rather than later."

He growls in annoyance. "No news, and I said I would tell you when there is something to tell."

"Why can't you just be a gentleman? You know, actually ask a woman if she would like to accompany your big ego to an evening for charity? I mean, wouldn't you want Hadley to only ever be *asked* by a man, so she knows she has a choice?"

Spencer hums a sound of disapproval. "Don't bring her into this, and fine, I'm sure I'll make it up to you."

"How the hell do you plan on doing that?"

His eyes linger down to my tits and then back up to my mouth. "Not tonight."

Disappointment floods inside of me, because for a second, I felt a need for what my imagination was playing in my head.

"Since this is my pool, I guess you should follow my swimming rules."

I scoff a sound. "Oh geez, what rule did I forget this time?"

His fingers are quick to land on the knot of my bikini top on my back where he tugs slightly and then stops. "Women whom I fuck only swim naked in this pool."

He pulls a little more.

I lean in to let our breaths mingle, an ache forming between my legs, but I want to have the upper hand. My lips barely trace his jawline.

"A shame that you only *fucked* me, past tense. Loophole of your rule," I whisper.

A devilish smirk forms on his mouth.

Tug.

My top falls loose and my nipples appear.

He hisses a sound. "Oh no," he says, feigning regret. "Accidents do happen."

I own this moment, and with purpose grab hold of the bikini top that is about to float away and throw it behind me onto the deck of the pool.

He moves closer, my clit beating against the movement of water for any relief that I can get.

"Do you know what I hate to admit?" He tips his head to the side, his breath hitting my neck.

"That you're a headache to the female population?" I breathe out, but it's shaky.

His fingertips trace the curve of my breast, and I feel my body shudder from his touch.

"I like when you're feisty, completely unreasonable, and a pain to have a normal conversation with."

"Who the hell enjoys that?" I wonder as my body molds into him.

He pinches my nipple. "The guy who has every intention of fucking you into compliance."

Spencer grips my hips and hoists my body up, my legs naturally floating to wrap around his waist where I feel his hard cock.

I bite my bottom lip because my hand weaves through his hair to guide his head down where he takes a nipple into his mouth, and I moan in approval.

All logic is slipping away, and I'm giving into this need that my body has, a void that only he can fill, caution thrown to the wind.

His lips pull away, but he traps my little bud between his teeth, and he playfully teases me. Looking down and I see him peering up at me.

The sound of his popping lips fills the room. "Get out of the pool, April," he demands.

I'm taken aback. "Excuse me?"

"Unfortunately for us, the friction of pool water is not in our favor. So, get the fuck out and walk slowly to the shower over there." He tips his head to the stone wall with a shower behind it, the kind of shower you see at a spa after the sauna.

"What makes you think I will comply?"

He's quick to loosen the ties on both sides of my bikini bottom in one go.

"I don't, but either way, you're pretty much as good as naked, so I already win. Now be a smart girl and get out of the pool."

His commanding voice is hard to resist, I admit.

He swims away and exits the pool, and I don't feel any resistance inside of me, so I slowly swim a few strokes to the steps and, with a cautious sway, get out and walk to the shower where he is already under the spray of water.

"The friction of water isn't in our favor, remember?" I retort.

He snags my wrists, yanks me forward, and turns us so my back is against the stone wall, with the shower over us. The whole move is kind of exhilarating.

"Pool water isn't. The shower is different."

He steps back, finishes the job of tugging my bikini bottom ties free, and throws the fabric to the side, leaving me naked. I should feel vulnerable, but he gives me the once-over, and I feel extremely turned on that he is assessing me like a prize. He reaches between us, and he hooks his finger to trace my pubic bone with a satisfied smirk.

"You always wax or just when you know that you want to fuck the guy whose house you're staying in?"

My eyes blaze with slight fury at his words. He never needs to know that I *may* have gone for a quick wax before I drove up here a few days ago.

"Here is how this is going to go, April. You will be by my side at that charity event."

"Oh gee, I don't have anything to wear," I counter with an excuse.

"I'll arrange that."

I roll my eyes. "Controlling."

"Nah, controlling would be telling you that you're not going to wear an ounce of fabric underneath the dress because we need you ready for every moment that I plan on punishing you for that mouth of yours that just runs wild with words."

"I feel like this is a one-sided dislike. You keep making it sound as though I'm the only one in our dynamic who hates when we're together," I say huskily as my mouth spars with his, trying to get a taste, but he denies me because taunting me is his game.

His fingertips travel up the side of my body as he presses his body into me. "Hate is a strong word, but damn, you are irritating. So irritating that I want to fuck you as a consequence."

"Spencer." My voice sounds more desperate than the warning that I intended.

He plants his long finger on my mouth to shush me. "The next time you open your mouth it better be to moan."

Dropping to his knees, he brings my leg over his shoulder and his mouth covers my center. His tongue instantly hits my clit, causing my body to bolt from the momentary relief.

I voluntarily rest my arms by my head against the wall, a sort of surrender.

Spencer is relentless in his pursuit of my pussy. Jesus, that tongue is a weapon.

I feel like I'm nearly unable to breathe, only made worse when I look down to see Spencer on his knees and on a mission. And despite the water cascading down our bodies, I'm not sure the warmth is helping, as my entire body is peaked with arousal. Little goosebumps appear on my skin, and I feel like my balance is about to be lost.

Especially when he adds a finger to the equation and works his way inside of me.

"Fuck, fuck, fuck," I mutter to myself.

His tongue finds a rhythm, and my lungs want to burst out of my chest because I can't breathe.

"Spencer," I attempt to say his name, but it comes out a long slew of letters. My hand lands on his shoulder so I don't fall.

Then he throws me off when he interlaces our hands against the wall, but he doesn't stop with his tongue. He keeps stroking me and making sounds like he's enjoying every millisecond.

I close my eyes as I melt into the feeling of being ravished. And they stay closed until I'm unraveling against his mouth, convulsing from the effect.

He stays on me until I seem to have calmed down before he slowly rises to stand, with the water the only sound between us, our eyes intense as we both visibly breathe out of pace.

I move to touch him, return the favor, but he stops me by grabbing my arm.

"Trust me, the stone wall won't be comfortable for the way I plan to fuck you. Good night, April." He runs his knuckles along my cheek before he is quick to step away, grab a towel, and disappear.

What in the world just happened?

I'm totally lost.

Because the next day, after avoidance, he surprises me when he returns home from picking Hadley up at school.

When I look at the kitchen counter, my blood boils yet again…

12

SPENCER

April looks like she is going to kill me.

I look between the bouquet of autumn orange roses that I left on the counter and April who is standing by the fridge, dumbfounded, her mouth parted open and her throat visibly gulping.

"What in the world?" Her eyes could drill a hole into the flowers.

My cheeky smirk comes out in full swing. "I'm doing what we call *listening*." I walk around the kitchen island and look over my shoulder at Hadley who I picked up from school and who is now eating a snack of donut bites. They have hidden zucchini and apples in it, and April conveniently left them out on a plate with a juice box, ready for Hadley's arrival.

April is thoughtful that way. It irks me, and not in a bad way either, but I can't focus on that feeling when a scowl sweeps across her face.

"Listening?" April approaches the flowers as if they might destruct.

I turn to Hadley. "You see, a guy should always *ask* if you would like to go somewhere, and sometimes they bring flowers to soften the deal. Then you should think about their offer, probably discuss it with your dad, and then give an answer."

"Huh?" My daughter just looks at me, uninterested, before popping another ball into her mouth.

"Yeah, what she said." April looks at me with hesitation.

Taking a few steps with confidence, I glue my sight on April, ensuring her bewildered eyes stay fixed on me. "Well, April, will you accompany me for this charity event?"

She straightens her neck and looks around the room. I have her trapped because Hadley is watching us, which is why her sight pauses on my daughter for a second before focusing on me.

"I think I'm missing a please." She cocks her head to the side.

Difficult, this one. My grin turns tight. "Will you *please* do me the honor of accompanying me to the charity event."

Now she smiles with accomplishment, one hand finding her hip and the other touching the roses. "Sure. Nice touch with the roses, by the way."

"Does this mean you get to dress up like a princess?" Hadley asks April.

April awkwardly hums a sound. "Depends on what your daddy has in mind, but I'm sure a potato sack wouldn't suffice."

"I don't know, gives good leg action," I mumble so only April can hear.

"Can I go watch TV?" Hadley is already swinging her legs off the stool.

"Sure. Take your snack with you," I suggest.

The moment Hadley turns her back to us, April's smile fades, and she points at me.

"You. Laundry room. Now." Her words sound seething.

Yet I follow her willingly, watching her feisty march and sway. When we get to the laundry room, she closes the door behind me, and she jabs her finger into my chest, sending a bolt of electricity down my spine.

"You're mocking me," she begins.

"What? Me?" I play coy.

"Yeah, you. You're taking my words from yesterday and mocking me. You didn't really want to get me flowers, you just wanted to prove a point," she loudly whispers, because she doesn't want Hadley to hear.

I swipe a hand across my jaw. "And? So what if I did? You get roses out of it."

"I now want to pull every petal off its stem to work out my absolute exasperation with you." Her hands come up in the air, as if she wants to throttle something.

"Exasperating?"

How am I the issue?

I step closer. "Heaven forbid you actually say thank you for the roses."

"No. To you? Absolutely not." She stares at me blankly before stepping closer. "You are the most confusing human on the planet."

"How so?" I'm slightly offended.

"You have no manners," she declares, with her hands gesturing with her words.

"Do explain."

She hisses, "Mocking me with flowers, going down on me last night. I mean, who does that? You didn't even kiss me."

And here I am in yet another predicament with this woman. Because around her she makes my control come undone. She makes my head spin when she opens her mouth, that I instantly find so incredibly sexy.

That mouth.

That fucking gorgeous mouth. It taunts me when she speaks and makes me go feral when it's shut.

She weakens me in a way that no man enjoys because it means she potentially has the power to wrap me around her little finger that is currently jabbing my shoulder.

"You're pissed that I didn't kiss your mouth?" I'm in awe that making her come on my tongue wasn't enough. I'm slightly offended too, as I thought my skills were way above exceptional. "That's what has you in a tantrum?"

"No." I swear a sound dings. It's a horrible lie.

Does this woman ever drop her defense? Wait, she has. A lot. And around me. First that night with the video, again when we watched it, and last night by the pool.

April just needs to be prodded like a bear and fucked like she could be everything.

In a snap decision, I grab her face, cradling her head with her chin in the palm of my hand.

"God damn it, April," I husk. I hear thick want in my voice, and I wonder if she notices. I feel a throbbing sensation in my chest, and her eyes have me lost in a daze similar to last night.

This keeps happening.

A need to touch her, tease her like no man has, challenge her the way she challenges me. All logic goes out the window when it comes to her. It's the attraction that's messing with me because nobody wants to sign up for her daily rants and raves.

And I normally do better by Hadley. I don't invite women into our lives, yet that's all I seem to do with April.

Her eyes penetrate my own with want.

A sound escapes from the back of my throat because there will be no more suspense in this moment.

I slam my mouth onto hers, and her sound of surprise vanishes when I draw in her breath. She gives in by kissing me back. I haven't kissed her since those months ago, yet still she tastes like cake, a distinct taste that I remember because I had spread it on her cheek.

Her murmur rumbles into my mouth as we struggle to pull our lips apart for a breath. But this isn't going to stop. We manage to take a quick inhale before our mouths seal together again. A rush takes over, and no thoughts come into my mind. I just give in to this moment.

April's arms loop around my neck, and I lift her up onto the washing machine that is conveniently on.

A laugh escapes, and she untangles our mouths, but her lips brush along mine. "Everything is vibrating," she whispers.

I grin to myself because she means the sensations from the machine, and hopefully what my lips do to her.

We go at it again, making out like two teenagers. Hands roaming, tongues dueling, and our mouths and necks getting thoroughly explored.

"Does this make up for yesterday?" I pant.

"Shh. I enjoy this more when you don't remind me of the reasons I don't like you." She doesn't elaborate because she kisses me again.

The height of the machine makes it perfect for her center to meet mine, and tilting my bulge into her, my hard cock must take her by surprise as she yelps and smiles against my jaw.

"I am trying to contain myself from ripping this sweater off of you," I warn. It's knitted, off-the-shoulder, and distracting.

She hums in approval.

This is a version of myself I don't quite recognize. Everything I do lately is the opposite of my structured rules and routine.

"April," my daughter calls out and seems to be walking down the hall.

Shit, Hadley.

April and I instantly freeze mid-kiss before I back away, swiping a hand through my hair.

"Yeah, kiddo?" April calls out and hops off the washing machine, quickly adjusting her shirt and glancing over her shoulder at me with a semi-panicked look, then her eyes dart down to my impressive member, and I turn away, my fist clenched in the air.

Hadley opens the door. "What are you doing in here?"

"Oh." April gulps. "Your dad was showing me how to turn on the washing machine."

With her hand clasping the handle, Hadley looks between us, skeptical.

"What did you need, sweet pea?" I ask, avoiding turning my full body to her.

"Can I walk Pickles?" she inquires with excitement.

Relief seems to flood April's face. "Sure. How about I come with you. Your dad mentioned he needs a cold shower or swim now anyhow." April begins ushering Hadley out, not even looking back.

When they're both out of sight, my hands land on the washing machine in frustration. I curse and growl because I let that moment happen.

I'm not even sure what has me in a mood more. The fact I kissed April while my daughter was in the other room so close, or the fact that Hadley interrupted us.

And both options are a problem.

Walking along the sidewalk in downtown Lake Spark, I take in the fact that it's getting colder outside. The cool air is needed, maybe it will snap me out of my mood. Since the laundry room entanglement the other day, April and I have done our best to avoid one another, only keeping to small talk when Hadley is around, as my daughter is, unbeknownst to her, a peacekeeper.

I only have half an hour before I need to pick up Hadley, but it would have been a wasted drive home only to turn around. Plus, I can imagine April is in the kitchen making something ridiculously delectable yet again. A quick stop at the drug store to pick up razors that I don't really need is clearly a more thrilling option.

Looking ahead, I notice a familiar tail and slow wobble. My eyes draw a line from Pickles up his leash to the blonde walking in my direction, her glare strong.

Clearly no escape or avoidance options on the table today.

"April." My short greeting is all I can manage. I'm not sure what to do.

"I wasn't expecting to see you here."

"I thought you would be back at the house. I'm running an errand while Hadley has tap class."

Pickles sniffs my leg and wags his tail, clearly happy to see me, and at least someone here is in a good mood.

April pulls him back slightly. "We don't like him, remember?" She's speaking to the dog.

Rolling my eyes, I'm reminded of why I never before placed April in the contender category. "Real adult."

Her eyes bug out at me, and her sound of disapproval flies off her lips that have a fresh coat of Chapstick, because, yeah, I fucking notice.

"Wow. You have some nerve. I mean, you are the king of mixed signals." She stalks forward with her shoulders puffing out and that damn finger pointing at me again. "Not that I would want any signal from you, other than that our video situation is solved and I can finally go on my return journey out of here."

I'm calling bullshit on this.

"Babe, that is the lie of the century. You have no problem following my signals, that's all you do."

"Don't call me babe," she growls.

Blowing out a breath, I prepare myself for this merry-go-round. "That's what you took away from that sentence?" Now I have to smirk. "Oh, right, you enjoy it when I'm in control, so you can only agree with everything I say."

"Spencer, your holier-than-thou baseball-player mindset is a real piece of work. You're the one initiating everything."

Now I chuckle under my breath, leaning into her space, close enough for our air to evaporate. "Nah, it's your mouth that gets us into these predicaments. Remind me to pick up a bar of soap when I hit the drug store."

"I much prefer tape when you want to get kinky," she jokes but in such a serious tone that she freezes when she realizes her error.

Chuckling to myself, I find this way too entertaining. I grab Pickles' leash from her hand, and she doesn't fight me as she just stews in her confession. And I don't mean the tape part; she admitted in non-plain terms that there will be another time.

I tug on Pickles' leash, and April peers down to watch him quite energetically walk closer to me.

"What are you doing with my dog?"

"He's coming with me."

"No, he's not," she volleys.

"Pickles is just living his life of Zen, remember? He suddenly has energy when he sees me."

"And squirrels. So congratulations, you are in the same category as squirrels," she states flatly.

Stepping dangerously close to April, I scan the scene to ensure nobody notices us before I speak in a low voice. "I'll take him back to the house. Hadley will love seeing him when I pick her up from dance. Besides, his owner needs to take a walk and cool down because she has to think about the fact that she still has to be my plus-one this week, and you best believe I'm going to make sure you look like the woman every guy wants to fuck but won't because they'll know you're there with me."

And I wouldn't need to do much because she already looks the part.

"What woman in their right mind falls for this shit you spew?"

I don't know, but you have me unable to think clearly.

I reach my finger out to tap the tip of her nose. "The one who is sleeping in my guest room because for one night she took a chance and decided I'm the guy she could have an adventure with."

"A nightmare. That's what this is." The line of her lips twists.

"Then why is a smile curling on your lips, and ten seconds ago, your hands found their way to my arms to hold, as if I'm the guy every woman wants to fuck but they won't because you're making a public claim."

Her eyes drop down to see that she is holding my wrists in an affectionate manner. She instantly drops my arms, and I hate that something feels absent.

"You will be a gentleman, a perfect gentleman tomorrow," she calls out a warning before turning to march away in a mood, leaving me to smile internally to myself.

She only marches a few steps before she makes a sharp turn to look at me. "We're acting insane."

"Completely." I can only agree, with my grin pulling on the corners of my mouth.

The hard line on her mouth disappears and a gentle smile begins to spread. "We always bicker."

"Isn't it fun?"

Her cheeks tighten because her smile only grows.

"Pizza tonight? I think Hadley will love to make her own pizza, and I can do a cauliflower crust so she has no clue she's eating a vegetable," she rambles as her temper from a minute ago fades into oblivion.

Hell, I'm no longer in the mood to spar. Not after she just made that offer for dinner.

"She will love that." And I do too.

One nod and then April begins to turn slowly, her smile not fading.

"You still better be a gentleman tomorrow," she reminds me with a little wave goodbye in the air.

"Still debating," I tell her, purely to keep the banter up.

But looking down at Pickles who wails a sound when he looks up at me, I know that every living creature can analyze this situation and see a fire.

A fire that I hate to admit, but I don't think I want to escape the flames.

13
APRIL

Well, this is ridiculous.

I look over my shoulder at my reflection in the long mirror.

"I'm not sure I should be wearing this," I mention as I take in the fact this long black dress is near backless which means no bra for me, especially as it ties around my neck.

"Spencer picked this out?" Piper asks for the tenth time as she sits at the edge of the guest bed, focusing between her baby girl lying on the mattress playing with a toy and staring at me in my predicament.

I can't tear my eyes away from the mirror. "This is not what I had in mind."

Piper smiles like a cat who found their prey. "The slit between your cleavage is a bold choice."

My eyes grow into saucers. "I know, right? But..."

Her smile grows wide. "You look smoking."

My own excitement comes out, especially because my updo is perfection. "I *do* look smoking."

This dress hugs me in all the right places, and it's a beautiful and very expensive dress. I'm not sure I want to know how Spencer managed to pick this out, he had to have enlisted someone's help. I feel like a million bucks.

I walk to the dresser to search for earrings. I hold up the long one and the stud for Piper's approval.

"Go simple," she suggests.

Studs it is.

I'm not quite sure why I have butterflies in my stomach, but this has been an unusual week, and I would be surprised if I didn't have nerves. The last few days have been unexpected.

It feels like a game with Spencer, yet I volunteer myself as tribute every round. Since our laundry room make-out the other day, we have basically ignored each other except when Hadley is around.

She is such a sweet little girl. Funny too. She gives Spencer a hard time, but at random moments does something to catch him by surprise in a way that I hope brings them closer.

"At least you will have fun at the charity dinner. It's for a good cause, to add a further addition to the new sports center where they'll hold summer camps for kids. If Hudson didn't have an away game this week then I'm sure we would be there too."

"It's kind of you to watch Hadley and Pickles. I guess we won't be that late."

"Don't sweat it. Unlike you, I have no problem with Spencer. I owed him a favor for the number of times he has signed for packages for me while I'm taking an impromptu nap."

I nod in understanding as I take a long breath to look at myself once more.

"You know…" I can tell Piper wants to point out the obvious. "You're Spencer's plus-one, people will see you together…"

"I'm just his plus-one," I reiterate.

"I doubt any cameras there will agree with that. But you don't seem to mind. Something you want to share?"

I focus on blending with my highlighter brush on my cheeks. "No." Because I don't know how to explain it.

"Just remember that you will one day find the guy who will erase all past mistakes. He'll be the magic you've been waiting for. So be it, he might not appear that way at first." She splays her hands out.

Before I can protest, I see Hadley in the corner of my eye arriving at my open door and walking straight to the dresser.

"Did you already put on the sparkly powder?" Hadley rummages through my makeup.

Of course, that's what she would be after.

"I did, but I can always use more." I take the case and brush, dab it in the powder, then offer it to Hadley and give her my arm to spread the stuff.

"Can you tell Daddy to let me have powder? When you're not here, I won't get to use this." She focuses on spreading the brush along my arm.

When I'm not here. Sometimes I forget that this is all temporary. I'm getting comfortable here, which should be a warning.

She hands me the brush in accomplishment, and I dab the brush on the cleavage line of my breasts without thought until Piper chortles a laugh.

"Interesting choice," she mutters.

Like a hot potato, I drop the brush back on the dresser because clearly, my subconscious is up to tricks.

"You look like a princess." Hadley smiles, and I can tell one of her front teeth is loose. I remember the conversation that I heard the other day between her and Spencer about the tooth fairy.

I stroke her hair with my hand. "Why, thank you." I pick up my clutch purse from the bed. "Now I just need to find my ogre," I mutter.

Walking out the front door, I feel my body fill with anticipation, but then I internally growl in irritation when I see Spencer leaning against the dark SUV, as he hired a driver for the night.

And I'm fuming inside because he is incredibly handsome.

He's in a tux, his hair slicked back, hands in his pockets, with a smirk on his mouth. Then he propels his body off the hood of the car, and he approaches me with swagger.

But the worst part?

His breath catches, and then he hisses a whistle of approval when he's a short distance away.

"You're late."

Ah, we are going to play this game.

"By two minutes because some baseball player apparently picked out a dress that involves a tie that acts as a lifeline for my cleavage."

"I approve." It feels like he is drinking me in.

I clear my throat. "You look..." How do I explain that I may drool?

"Everyone will be looking at you, and I might be regretting my choice now. Should have gone for the turtleneck option."

A wry smile doesn't leave my face. "Well, you did want me to look fuckable, as you put it in your ever charming terms."

"Nah, you look way classier than that. Come on, we should go." He offers me his arm. I'm slightly taken aback by his manners, but I interlink our arms anyway.

A whiff of his spicy cologne hits me, but it's enough to make my senses melt. His arm feels strong, and I need to get used to it because I think I'll be glued to him for most of the night.

By the time we're in the car and on our way, I recognize that the air between us has shifted; we're easy around one another.

I decide to break the ice. "Looks like the tooth fairy will be in business soon. Hadley's front tooth looks loose."

"I noticed that." An elated look spreads on his face. Spencer taps his fingers on his thighs as he looks out the window until he turns back at me. "How's the food blog?"

"I'm stockpiling recipes and photos, thanks to your kitchen. A total opposite to my life as an accountant."

"Good. That's good."

We don't seem to know how to handle this new dynamic between us, probably because we can't define it.

"New sports camp, huh?" I attempt to keep the conversation flowing.

"Yeah, it would be good for Lake Spark. Once I retire, then I'll have something to do."

"But you don't like kids except your own," I point out the obvious.

He rolls a shoulder back. "Doesn't mean I don't recognize that it's good for the community, or maybe I want to work with teenagers."

Oh my, I was not expecting that response.

"You'll retire soon?"

"I probably have one or two more good years, then I'll need to do something. I don't think coaching is for me."

"It does generally require interacting with people," I state.

He gives me side-eye. "Funny." His jaw eases. "I would like to spend more time with Hadley."

"Of course." I lean against the window, taking in the fact that I'm dressed to the nines and sitting with Spencer whose hardened exterior feels softened. I try to remember the last time I was at a black-tie event with a man. My soured feeling must be apparent because I feel like Spencer has a sneer forming.

"You okay?"

"The last time I went to an event like this, I was with my ex. It was his firm's Christmas gala." I puff out a breath. "Truthfully, I didn't have the best of times. He was all work and forgot about me most of the night."

"Nothing I've heard about this dude has been positive."

"Now, no. Sometimes we get stuck in the idea of something and ignore that we might not be with the right person to make it happen," I explain. Because I don't think my ex was the one; I'm mostly bitter because I felt humiliated.

Spencer adjusts in his seat, even slides closer to me. "You mean, your dream wedding?"

I narrow my eyes at him because I'm not sure if he's mocking me. "Enough about me. Am I going to run into any of your exes tonight?"

"None of my exes are from around here."

"Oh? But I do believe you have the 'women who you screw in your pool are only naked' rule."

He grins a pretty damn swoony grin. "April, sweetheart, you're the first in my pool."

I'm not sure why it hasn't crossed my mind, the idea of other women in his house, maybe because I assumed he has had special guests since he has so many options when it comes to women, or perhaps I've been too focused on the moment. That's a change, as I'm always thinking about the dream ahead or something that happened in the past; it's never in that moment, except when Spencer is around.

A tickle at my hip bone breaks my thought, and I peer down to find a talented finger tracing a line. Spencer is touching me of his own accord.

"A problem?" I raise my brows.

A smug accomplished smirk slowly appears. "You're wearing fabric underneath."

"Wow, he observes."

"You know in baseball when I pitch, I'm restricted to certain types of throws. It's actually rigid and doesn't leave me much choice, I have to stick to the program. Don't get me wrong, it's still exciting, or rather there are other ways to make a game interesting. For example, I could try to pitch an entire game to get a shutout, ensuring the other team doesn't score at all, and by end of game, my team wins. Want to know what I think?"

His lips brush along my bare shoulder like a feather, and a tingle runs through me. I pray my nipples don't give me away.

"That I need a sweater," I quip.

He chuckles, and I love how it's a sound that pulls me in and feels like an enticing offer.

"I think tonight will be like a shutout. I have no intention of letting anyone else score."

"Ah, but one problem." I rest my hand on his thigh, playing the part of a doting other half. "You won't get your homerun or whatever baseball term I should be using, because I may look the part, but I'm not in the mood to be fucked like you hate me."

His face is unreadable, but his jaw ticks, and I'm surprised he doesn't have a jab in return.

The car slows down, and glancing outside, I see we have apparently reached our destination, the sports center, with an outside marquee with heaters, thankfully.

When the car stops, Spencer gets out, buttons his tux, and leans back in to take my hand and help me out.

But as I stand and straighten my dress, the man leans in to whisper in my ear as he wraps a protective arm around my middle to bring my body to his, my upper half molding into his shape.

"Listen, beautiful, think what you want, but I'm not going to let anyone else score, so get used to being by my fucking side."

14

SPENCER

Why can't I stop watching her?

All night, I've kept my word, and April hasn't left my side. Instead, I've played a part that I'm not exactly used to... Prince Charming.

I fill her glass with wine when it needs a refresh, I keep my arm permanently on the back of her chair as we watch the auction, and I listen with a keen ear when she talks to the table about her trip to Italy and adopting a dog.

April wanted gentlemanly and I'm giving it, but I'm not sure why I care so much. Probably because this woman is possessing my thoughts.

"I'll be back." April breaks my moment of being lost in my head.

"Huh?"

"Ladies' room. I'll be back. Am I allowed, dear master?" she taunts me, clearly entertained. I stand up to help her pull her chair back, and her eyes turn strange. "Who are you when you wear a tux?" She seems astonished, and quite frankly, so am I.

"Cute. Real cute. I just believe I'm obeying your request that I be a gentleman tonight."

She hums a response before swaying away, just as Ford is walking back to our table and holding out a glass of scotch for me.

"You are completely enamored." Ford smirks to himself before taking a sip of his own glass.

We both sit down.

"She may be getting under my skin a little," I admit. Assessing the area, everyone is busy eating desserts and sipping wine. There are a few sports stars here, but in true Lake Spark fashion, it's the town mayor who takes center stage.

"I would be worried if she wasn't. Besides, she looks completely into you. It's funny watching you two together, like two teenagers with a crush."

"Come on, Ford, it's not that bad. Besides we're just comfortable around each other since she is staying at my place." I lean back in my seat and stare into my filled tumbler.

"And why is she staying with you? Oh yeah, because she already took a ride with you, consequences be damned."

I flash him an unamused look. "Enough about me. Why are you here solo? Wasn't the memo to bring a plus-one?"

His brows raise, as if he's surprised I asked, as I should realize the answer. "You know I don't bring dates to my home turf. It wouldn't feel right."

Biting the corner of my mouth, a wave of empathy hits me. I'm an ass for asking, because he treats Lake Spark like holy ground, as it's where he had his first real love and heartbreak, and if he had his way, then Brielle Dawson would also be his only love.

"How are you going with that?" I wonder.

He sighs a breath. "I see her every few weeks for ten minutes to discuss our boy and that's it."

I slap a hand on his back. "It'll work its way out. Besides, hockey season is about to start and will keep you busy."

"Thank fuck for that." He tips his head in the direction of the exit. "April is back. You're good if I ask her to dance?"

Shooting him a warning glare, it causes him to chuckle.

I slide out of my chair and quickly charge a few steps to meet April halfway, and in a flash, I loop an arm around her middle.

She startles from surprise. "What in the world?"

"Let's dance."

"Really?" She seems skeptical. "You dance?" But she doesn't protest and follows me to the dance floor where a slow song is playing.

A faint smile graces her lips when our eyes meet as we face one another, her arms finding a home around my neck as we move our bodies to the music.

"How was your temporary escape?" I joke.

"Not bad. Listening to the old ladies debate if the hockey player or baseball player is better suited for their granddaughter was absolutely amusing, especially when they realized I was standing there in line."

I relax into this moment. "You're the threat, clearly." I feel my phone vibrate in the front pocket of my suit. "Sorry, let me quickly check that in case it's Hadley related."

April's eyes have a sort of admiration hinted in them; they sparkle, but that's probably the light. "Absolutely."

Reaching into my tux jacket, I slide out my phone and see that Piper texted. I swipe my thumb across the screen, and I can only internally celebrate the development.

"Everything okay?"

"Yeah." I tuck the phone back into my tux. "Piper took

Hadley and Pickles back to her house, as the baby needed an extra change of clothes. Hadley is going to sleep there tonight since it's easier."

"Lies, I tell you. There is no way that baby needed an extra change. Piper never leaves her house without at least three outfits for the kid." April laughs.

Sounds about right. Piper did insert a winking emoji that I didn't tell April about.

"Ah well, we are now in no rush or anything." I pull April flush since I feel like I can let go tonight without restrictions.

"Or anything," April barely echoes in a whisper.

It makes me scoff, as I like where her mind goes. "Having a good time despite being stuck with me?"

"Actually, this is kind of fun. Thank you for insisting I be your plus-one against my will." She clicks the inside of her cheek with her tongue.

"I brought you flowers," I remind her.

"You did, and you paid an exorbitant amount for the private chef at the Dizzy Duck for one night in the auction. I may soften my stance on you if you let me be your plus-one for that so I can assess if it's a good menu."

I twirl her around. "I think you've already softened your stance on me."

"Maybe true," she replies point blank, and her honesty catches me off guard.

I bring her hand to rest against my chest, near my heart that has been prodding me lately. "You would want to go back to the Dizzy Duck with me?"

"It is a dangerous location, but I do what I must for good food and conversation."

"So now I'm good at conversation too?" I tease her.

She playfully swats my chest. "Sometimes. Outside of Hadley and baseball, you're still kind of a mystery to me."

"Really? What do you want to know?"

"Hmm, what would you do if you didn't play baseball?"

I try to suppress my grin. "I only know baseball, but I'm not blind that at any moment it could all end, so I guess in the back of my mind, I would want to invest in a hotel or something. I studied business in college."

"Okay, I guess that's straightforward. Can I ask something else?" She focuses on her finger playing with the button on my white shirt. I nod. "Why are you so… unapproachable to most?"

I chortle a laugh. "Wow. Are you asking why I'm grouchy? I'm not always. I just worked hard to get to where I am, I need to be focused. My parents didn't have much, I wasn't handed a silver spoon, but now I can have it all. And besides, what went down with Hadley… I have every reason to keep people at bay." A ping deep within my heart aches.

"I get it, and I'm not going to say sometimes we need to move on to new chapters and try again. I've seen people at their worst too."

"Their loss."

"I think so," she agrees.

We dance in place, swaying, our eyes piercing in a locked gaze. Inside, I feel an internal battle; the fact I kept the video, yet I'm thankful I did, otherwise we wouldn't be here.

"You don't hate me, do you? Like really hate me because I kept the video?"

Her chin tips up as she breathes a long breath. "Detest isn't hate. And… I don't know. Is it strange that I'm not mad? Fine. I admit it. I'm not that mad. A little nervous the whole world may see it, but at least I can say it led me on an adventure, with an added bonus of benefitting from your kitchen."

I debate what to say next but settle on simple. "I can live with that." In the corner of my eye, I notice the floor clearing, and then it dawns on me that the music is fading. "We should probably head back."

"Yeah, a good idea."

I strip off my jacket to drape on her shoulders, and she gives me a peculiar look. "You gave me the standard of being on good behavior, remember? Plus, you must be freezing."

"I think you wanted it that way."

We begin to walk side by side, our arms grazing. "Why would that be, April?"

"Because you like when I suffer, despite whatever is going on in that head of yours, and I'm fairly confident that your mind is going wild." She is sure of herself, and she isn't far off.

The only clear point in my brain right now is that I feel lucky tonight.

Looking out the floor-to-ceiling living room window, I glance at the stars while I drink a nightcap. My tie hangs loose around my neck.

We had a silent ride back, and the moment we stepped inside the house April disappeared. Fair enough. I haven't touched her to prove a point. I could have slipped my fingers between the slit of her dress to feel her wet and ready, but I refrained because I knew that was what she was expecting.

Now, I'm taking a moment to relish the fact that Hadley isn't here, because off-season, I don't have many breaks from being a dad, and during baseball season, I have no breaks from being a star pitcher. It's all one continuous grind.

"Hey, can you help with this?" I hear April approaching behind me.

Turning halfway, I see she is indicating to the zipper that

conveniently rests on her lower back, causing the dress to become a second skin to the curve of her ass.

Smirking to myself, I know what she is trying to do, but I'll play along.

"Come here," I say and set my drink on the side table.

April slowly turns in front of me, offering her back, and my fingers willingly find the zipper to tug, but I pause. Instead, I inhale her flowery perfume and feel bold.

"I'll help you, but you have to do something for me."

"What?"

"Take off your panties."

I'm far too curious if my theory is correct.

She throws me a coy look over her shoulder, hesitating at first, but quickly skims the bottom of her dress up her silky legs and reaches under to pull down the black thong. It slides down her legs, and she steps out of them, holding them up for presentation.

I grab my prize, and my smirk of accomplishment is immediate. "My, my, someone has been soaking." The fabric feels damp, and I bring it to my nose, her distinct smell as sweet as I know she tastes. Her lips part open as she watches me.

"Will you help me now?" Her brows arch.

I step closer to her, and I'm quick to shove the ball of panties into her mouth. She mumbles something from surprise but doesn't spit them out. "Now I will." My smirk is now cocky.

My fingers return to her zipper, and I pull slowly down, feeling the softness of her sparkly powdered skin and the firmness of the curve of her body. The fingers of my other hand entwine in her hair to find any form of a clip, then I slide it out, which is followed by her hair falling loose around her shoulders.

"If you're going to play the game then go all in with your efforts," I suggest.

She glances over her shoulder with a wicked look and spits out the fabric. "Wishful thinking." With purpose, she brings her arm to the bow at the back of her neck, tugging, before her arms come forward to shield her breasts as the fabric hangs loose around her body.

"Night, night. I need to go hang this up, as this dress is prone to wrinkles."

She walks away, clearly satisfied with her performance, and I watch every step as she fades out of the room.

Blowing out a deep breath, I take one last sip of my drink to calm me then scoop up the destroyed thong.

I want the upper hand, and I will not go after her. Challenging April is the highlight of my day lately, and that means not doing what she would expect. I'll just take a shower and go to bed.

Simple as that.

FIVE MINUTES LATER, I'm in my bathroom unbuttoning my shirt, waiting for the water in the shower to warm up, yet I can't seem to commit. Physically, I don't want to step under the stream to find relief.

Not when the best release is a few doors down.

What the fuck am I doing?

Everything inside me is going crazy for this woman. All week, I've wanted to lead, but the truth is, she has the ability to make me follow. To make me not use rational thought. Hell, I've invited her into my home and interwoven April into Hadley's life. I'm not the type of guy who thinks of a future with someone, but if I think of tomorrow then April is in every second of it.

This is frustratingly new. I should be mad at her just for that.

Fuck it.

I turn the water off, and in a full-speed walk, I head straight to April's room. Opening the door without a knock, I stand in the doorway to find her sitting in the middle of the bed, leaning against the headboard in sexy little pajama shorts and my old team t-shirt that she must have cut because it's hanging off her shoulder and doesn't go an inch below her belly button. The smirk on her face is like she won the World Series.

She was waiting for me.

"There you are." She plays coy, pretending to examine her nails. "A minute longer than I predicted."

I shake my head, and my genuine smile from this situation spreads. I storm to her bed, take hold of her ankles, and pull her to the edge of the mattress. She squeals in approval.

"No fucking way we are doing this here. We're heading to my bedroom," I tell her before throwing her over my shoulder.

15

SPENCER

Throwing April on my bed, I don't question why I had a primal urge to take her to my room, but the guest room just wouldn't do.

April leans back on her elbows to assess me as I stand at the edge of the bed.

"I guess you've never been in here," I note as I slowly bring one knee to the mattress and then the other.

A sly grin appears on her lips as she comes up to sitting, her hands splaying against my searing skin, pressing my chest for a feel. "Silly boy, I snooped around here days ago. Even stole a shirt, in case you didn't notice." She yanks my unbuttoned dress shirt down my arms before returning to lying on my bed.

"Oh, I noticed." One arm lands on the side of her and our eyes cling to one another. I glare a warning before my other arm finds a spot near her shoulder to cage her underneath me.

"No pressure or anything, but you did say the other day that you would fuck me so hard that a stone wall just wouldn't do, and lucky me, there seems to be a mattress this time." Her sultry tone is toying with me.

I growl from her playfulness, a refreshing change to our fiery exchanges during all our previous rounds. Slamming my lips down onto hers, I make it clear that I have every intention to take her the way I've been wanting to for days.

I dip my tongue into her mouth, and she purrs a sweet sound that makes me eager to kiss her harder.

Her pointed foot travels up my leg until it lands on my ass, opening her up wide to me, and I'm ready to lose my mind.

"I have no intention of going slow with you."

"Good, we are to the point," she jokes against my lips.

My hand roams her body, wanting to touch her everywhere yet unsure where to focus. April seems to be in the same predicament, as her hands mimic my own.

"I should spank you for looking so ridiculously beautiful tonight, then fucking blowing my mind by wearing my shirt."

"What if I jinx your team?" she one-tones.

I chuckle as I drag my lips down the soft skin of her neck. "I'll take the chance." She tugs at my belt. "Don't tell me you've practiced," I warn her before taking over to finish the job.

There is a glint in her eye. Her breathing is different, like maybe she wants to say something but doesn't. Instead, the moment I'm over her again after removing my pants, she sneaks into the waistband of my boxer briefs, and her fingers wrap around my length. I close my eyes and let out a sound of agreement.

April isn't afraid to lead, but that's not how I roll. But damn, her hand feels good on me.

"We need to get there faster," she coos.

I begin to yank down her little shorts as she does mine, and we both pause in our fast chaotic movements to finish the task of removing layers. I'm quicker, and it gives me the opportunity to pin her wrists against the mattress as my other hand heads straight to the only place I want to be this evening.

Feeling between her folds, the warmth of her juices causes me to hiss, as she is ready. Finding her little bead, I rub her arousal in a circular motion against her clit. Another finger drives into her center, and I feel her tightness. It made me near delirious the other day when I went down on her.

Maybe I've essentially been gearing her up all week, yet I can't help but wonder. "Why are you so tight, April?" I study her face as her breath catches and my finger continues to work her. I can't lie, I love having control over her.

"You know that answer," April whispers, and I could swear I hear vulnerability.

She doesn't give me a clear response, so I stop my effort to bring her to her edge. I walk my fingers up her flat stomach and underneath the flimsy shirt, and I find a nipple to pluck. "You haven't been with anyone since our video escapade," I point out the fact.

Her tongue darts out to lick her lips. "Have you?"

I smirk to myself; I have no problem admitting the obvious. "Don't read into it. I don't fuck random people during baseball season." If she can do the math then she knows that she was my last.

She figures it out, because she leans up, wraps her arms around my neck, and pulls me into a kiss. A passionate kiss that shows she enjoys our truths, and hell, I kind of agree with her.

We draw our kiss out until the need for air hits us.

It's intoxicating how lost I am in this moment. We both want me to plunge right into her, and we can't get there quick enough because our mouths and hands run wild.

Proven by the fact that she rolls me to my back and straddles me with a confident look before she ensures I'm watching her peel the shirt up and off her body, revealing her beautiful tits. I smile as I reach to my nightstand table for a foil package before I flip her right onto her back again and coax her to shimmy up the mattress until her head rests on a pillow.

I part her legs wide, diving in to place my mouth on her heat, kissing her inner thighs, blazing a trail of determination in the process. I lick her once, twice, but that's all she will get because we have one goal right now.

Crawling up the mattress to cage her in, I breathe near her ear, her hair extra flowery, and I hate her for the fact that it will linger on my pillows.

"Wrap those pretty little legs of yours around my waist," I urge.

"I'm always, what was it you said…" She pretends to search for a word. "Compliant." April tilts her hips up against me to highlight her efforts.

I sheathe the condom on. "The thing about this scenario is that I've worked you up all week so this round we don't need to be gentle."

A lazy smile appears on her lips as I tease the tip of my cock around her opening, gliding between her slick heat, taunting her clit, entering her without warning then backing out.

My finger does one more test round, exploring her, and she yelps in surprise when I touch her intimate back opening. A sinister hum escapes me. "Relax. We'll explore that another round."

Her eyes grow wide before her delicate long finger circles my shoulder while I align myself with her opening. "You keep referring to rounds, plural?" She cocks a brow.

Driving myself in until I reach her hilt, we both gasp from

the force. "Okay, multiple rounds," she breathes out in agreement and gets lost in the feeling of me filling her up.

I pull out only to push back in, doing it a few times until I feel April ease underneath me.

Our eyes hold as I move inside of her, until a few pumps later, when our foreheads touch and we slow the pace.

Slowing it down makes this far worse. I'm sinking into her, wanting to drag out every second of this because she feels like the best thing that could ever happen between the sheets. I was never meant to play any sport but baseball, and now I think I may not be meant to fuck anyone but April.

That frustrating point causes me to fuck her with a bit more force, hooking my arms under her knees to draw them up toward my shoulders, her body willingly offering itself to me.

Her warm wet pussy that is as good as her snide remarks.

The sound of skin slapping and our heavy breathing fills the room. I feel heat spread throughout my body, and I notice the blissful look on April's face.

I peer down to get a glimpse of my cock sliding into her, and it's a magnificent view. But not quite as good as April's mouth in an O shape, with her breath trapped because she is lost in the feeling of having me inside of her.

"Breathe," I remind her.

"Fuck," she bluntly replies.

A laugh escapes me as I continue her request.

My finger lands on her clit to bring her to the next level, but truthfully, the next few minutes are a blur because our mouths continue to fuse, and we keep turning the tide with slow, fast, slow, fast until her teeth are clenching into the corner of my mouth as I bring her to her edge.

"Spencer." My name on her lips sounds like a plea, one that I ignore because I want her undone.

Her shaking and trembling while I'm inside of her is the only way that I'll accept this, and it's what happens as she quivers and her breath turns ragged.

I slow my strokes and look down at her face, softening as she comes down from her orgasm, and when I know she's ready, I continue to pump into her to bring me to my own release. It doesn't take long.

Short and fast was how this was going to go. It's the only way when you've been torturing one another for days.

I feel the sensation travel from below my navel and to my cock before I unload into the condom. April's heat wraps tightly around my length.

"Shit," I say as I fall forward, holding my weight so I don't crush April, but I rest my head against hers for a moment.

She rakes her nails along my back as we both lie on my bed in a stew of our own bizarre attraction.

And I have enough experience to know that when you enjoy the seconds after the climax just as much as the main event, then you have a situation.

Because right now, I don't want to leave this bed.

16
APRIL

I want to strangle him as much as I want to kiss him.

It's unfair because the all-night stamina of an athlete is something that I'm unable to compete with.

He has me on my side, back to him, and my arms stretched out over my head as he pumps into me, and he doesn't go easy or sweet. Yet, I'm completely relaxed, and I sink into another round of ecstasy because Spencer somehow knows how to take care of my body.

Sounds escape my mouth, creating my own original tune, my body jolts on every deep thrust, and his lips placing a kiss on my shoulder blade is probably the real cause of my undoing that hits me in a wave.

"Good girl," he grits out as he holds my hip down and continues his quest.

"Spencer," I purr because I hate that he teases me with that phrase.

He follows me shortly after, and I don't look over my shoulder when I feel him slide out of the bed. Instead, I lie in *his* bed, completely spent.

When he emerges from his bathroom, I can't help but take

in the scene of him naked. A freaking sculpture of perfection, right down to his endowment size. Such a shame these qualities didn't spill over into his personality. I smile to myself because that's not true either; I'm peeling away his layers.

"What's on your mind?" he asks as he works his way back into bed.

"Nothing. My brain can't function because I've been fucked all night." I pull the covers up a little higher, and I'm not sure why.

Spencer yanks the sheet back down slightly before he lies on his side and props his head against an elbow. "It's going to be a little rough this morning. We barely slept, and Piper will bring Hadley home soon."

I wince from the thought. Now I can relate to Piper and her lack of sleep and need to still parent.

"Some days are pretty brutal. Kids aren't afraid to speak without a filter and will point out your faults whether you are well-slept or not."

"At least you only have to deal with it for half of the year." The moment it slips off my lips, I feel horrible, especially when I see the hurt in his eyes. Instantly I reach out to touch his arm. "I'm sorry. I didn't mean for it to come out like that."

"Yeah, you did." He sounds somber.

"Okay, maybe in the literal sense, but not in the 'you're a douchebag' sense," I try to assure him.

He blows out a breath. "It's fine. Let it go."

"Is it? I mean, here, I'm giving you a free pass. Take a dig at me." I pat his arm with the suggestion. "Remind me that I only date boring doctors and lawyers who never make it past the first date."

Spencer smirks to himself before getting more comfortable in his position. "That's only a plus for me, April. It means your pussy is molded to my cock."

I ruefully shake my head, because of course he will take us back to vulgar talk. Flopping back to rest my head on the pillow, I blow out an exhausting breath.

A few beats of silence grace the room, and I take the moment to recall the night. I feel the smile on my lips then pause when the obvious hits me.

"*So*, this, well…"

Spencer looks at me, patiently waiting for me to finish the sentence, and he seems entertained. "Go on," he insists.

I swallow. "Piper will be here soon; I should probably go shower and make breakfast."

"Why would you need a shower?" he says, playing dumb.

I toss a spare pillow at him. "You know why."

He blocks the pillow and manages to take hold of my arms to bring me into his embrace as he rests against the headboard. "You're sore?"

"I don't know. I'm debating if my center of gravity has changed."

Spencer chuckles and wraps me tighter. "If it hasn't then let me know and I'll fuck you in the pantry later for good measure."

I slap his arm and then decide to test the boundaries by intertwining our fingers. "So last night," I return to my earlier attempt to bring some clarity to the situation.

"It is what it is," he comments with no hint of where his mind is at.

"Right." That's my cue to slip out of bed and find some clothes.

I begin to do just that, and as my ass is about to slide off the bed, I hear him sigh and grab my arm.

My eyes dart to his hand on my elbow, then my sight pivots up to meet his steely gaze.

"I'm not the guy to be more than this," he says.

"Just a little hate sex, we've been here before," I brush it off.

His cheeks raise and his mouth quirks. "Last night wasn't hate sex. If it was then I would have pulled your hair a little more and bit you somewhere visible just to annoy you that you wouldn't be able to forget me until the mark fades."

That's actually quite a turn-on. "Rain check then."

"To my utter dismay, you're getting under my skin in a way that I'm not used to."

Fear that he may have regretted last night fades, and my body softens into his words. "Likewise."

"Something is shifting."

"I agree." I can't blink, and nerves now hit me, the kind you get when someone catches your eye and takes an interest, except this time it's a heavier feeling, more intense.

"I have nothing else to offer right now except that you're staying here in this house, Hadley adores you—"

"Don't sweat that. If I didn't have Pickles then I would be completely boring to her." I do my best to downplay the situation.

He smiles gently at my attempt to reassure him. "Can we just leave it as we had a good night together?"

"Sure." I avoid his gaze.

"And I'll confess that there may be a tiny little hope that you sneak your cute ass right back in here tonight." Ah, there is his cocky look.

That grin of his stretches, and I feel my own subtle hint of a smile returning, especially when I look down to see that he hasn't let my fingers go.

And for now, that's good enough.

"You know, this screams that you are trying to cover something up." Spencer grabs a piece of fruit from my bowl.

Scanning all the dishes I just prepared, I guess he has a point. A simple breakfast somehow turned into waffles, fruit salad, eggs, bacon, and I even have donuts in the oven that I'll roll in cinnamon sugar later.

In truth, I'm a little nervous. Mostly because I know it's obvious to Piper what must have happened last night, and I don't want Hadley to think something is different.

"I guess I should have stuck to coffee and your protein shake laced with superpowers, but I got distracted," I admit.

Spencer runs his hand up my spine, and my body shivers in delight.

I enjoy a few seconds before I shake him off. "Down, boy, I need to recover, and besides, I think daylight may be highlighting my wrong life choices." I give him a stern eye.

"Your body says something else." His eyes dip down to my nipples that are peaked under my t-shirt. I'm quick to fold my arms over my chest for cover.

The sound of the door opening catches our attention. A mixture of paws on wood, a baby cooing, and Hadley running in.

"Yoo-hoo, I come bearing gifts," Piper announces as she walks into the kitchen holding up a box from Jolly Joe's in one hand, and she's balancing Gracie on her other hip. Pickles pads along beside Hadley. Piper's smile drops to confusion when she sees the buffet laid out on the kitchen island. "Oh. Clearly someone needed to be occupied this morning." She flashes me an overdone smile.

Spencer gives me knowing eyes as he walks to his

daughter who just hopped up on a stool. "I'm not hungry," Hadley declares.

"There are donuts in the oven," Spencer informs her.

"Still not hungry."

He grabs her a plate and dishes up some fruit anyways. "Well, I'm sure you'll change your mind." He turns to Piper. "Thanks for watching her, I owe you one."

"It's all good. I let her play dress-up and she helped me with the bambino. You two look absolutely tired," Piper points out, sneaking in a smirk as she sips from her to-go cup.

"It was a late night. I mean, the charity thing." My fingers fumble in the air.

Her chortle causes Spencer and me to glance at one another, as Piper is onto us.

Snapping, I bite the bullet. "Piper, a word in the other room, please." I smile tightly.

She looks giddy. Without even asking, she hands her baby over to Spencer.

He is quick to protest. "I don't do babies."

"Sure, you do. You're a pro. Thanks, you're a doll." She ignores him and nearly skips to the end of the hall.

When I arrive at the door near the garage, she has a golden smile, with her arms crossed over her chest.

"Just tell me you didn't make another video," she requests.

I shake my head.

"The 'I had a good time last night' look does great things for your complexion," she comments.

I roll my eyes, and as much as I pretend to be annoyed, I erupt in a joyful sound and grin. "Can we forget this?"

"No, because I want you to wake up and accept that your shitty dating life lately might be solved with a guy who knows how to throw a fastball."

Quickly I interject, "It's nothing more than physical."

"Sure, it is." She's certain. "Listen, just don't get hurt, and also be open. I honestly don't know what to make of this situation other than wow, you look like you're enjoying life for the first time in a long time. He's a good distraction." She affectionately touches my arm. Quickly, she gives me a hug. "Okay, we're not going to overstay our welcome."

She begins to walk away, and I call out her name. "Have you not seen the kitchen counter? Please stay."

Piper waves me off. "Nah, I'm sure Spencer worked up a big enough appetite." She winks before continuing her path.

She leaves me there in reflection that indeed for the first time in a long time, I'm having fun and smiling, and it isn't forced.

THE REST OF THE DAY, Spencer played with Hadley. He took her to the playground in town, while I stayed at the house because I needed to work on a paper for my nutritional course. I'm so close to being finished, and then I can start applying for jobs because a successful blog may be wishful thinking, but at the very least, it takes time to grow.

A knock on my door disrupts my focus on the screen. Looking up, I find Spencer casually leaning against the doorframe, t-shirt hugging his muscles, and my eyes enjoy the view.

"Checking to see if I threw out my vibrator?" I wisecrack.

He slowly steps into my room. "I already destroyed that a few days ago since you won't be needing it."

I tilt my head to the side before I lean on the side table and pull open the drawer. I bite my inner cheek because the devil actually did it, and I didn't notice because he has been fulfilling my needs in that department, from that night in the pool to last night.

"You owe me a new one when I return to the city." I set my laptop to the side and scooch forward and off the bed to meet him in the middle of the room.

"About that." He swipes a hand across his jaw, struggling to bring his thoughts together.

Immediately, my fear surfaces. "Oh God. The video, it's leaked?! Shit, I need to text my mother." I begin to pace the room. "My uncle may kill you. Let's say goodbye to my future job prospects too. Then there is my spiteful ex who will not let me forget this, I'm sure," I ramble, but a strong arm stops me.

"April." Spencer's voice is calm, and he cradles my head between the palms of his hands, the print of his thumb dragging along my bottom lip. "It's fine. We're fine. No longer an issue."

"Oh."

"Lawyer did wonders, and the file is deleted, all traces gone."

Well, that's... great. It should be fantastic. But why do I feel deflated? Oh, right, because that means...

"I guess I'm no longer a prisoner here." I sound disappointed.

His jaw flexes side to side. "True."

Neither one of us seem to know what to say. I glance over my shoulder. "I guess I'll pack up and head back—"

"Stay," he blurts out.

"Stay?"

Tone down the hope, April. Geez.

Spencer shrugs a shoulder as he runs the back of his knuckles along my cheek. "Yeah, I mean, you need my kitchen, right?"

His kitchen?

"It is a great kitchen."

The subtle hint of a grin tells me that it's code language for finding a reason that isn't obvious he wants me to stay.

Stepping closer to him, I roll my lips in, confident with my theory. "I do have a lot I still need to do, recipes, of course."

He stands taller and inches closer. "Settled then."

"Uh-huh."

Our mouths of their own accord move to trace one another's lips, but neither one of us dares to commit. A simple brush of our lips is enough for this moment, the hint that something bigger is underlying. Neither one of us could be that blind to ignore it.

"A few extra days wouldn't hurt. I mean, I'm sure you can tolerate me for that long," I whisper.

A soft rumble leaves his mouth. "Something like that." He bops his finger on the tip of my nose before giving me a subtle smirk as he turns to leave.

I watch him go as a swirling feeling of excitement and fear travels through me, because Spencer Crews is turning out to be everything I never imagined him to be.

17

SPENCER

She shakes her booty in my kitchen. That's what April does when she thinks nobody is watching, and she's focused on her latest creation. She keeps her ear pods in and dances around. I even caught her in full-on down-to-the-floor moves while she sang "It's Tricky" by Run DMC. She had no idea I caught her until she turned around.

But today, I return from dropping Hadley off at school to find April rocking her hips as she swirls a wire whisk in a bowl, unaware that I'm back.

The moment my hand rests on her lower back where I'm standing behind her, she's startled at first, until she melts into my touch.

"Hmm, I thought you had a meeting with a sponsor." She wiggles against me.

"Canceled," I whisper into her ear.

April slowly turns to look at me. "Oh, so you thought you would pencil me into your calendar for a workout?" She gives me a warning glare.

It's been a few days since I asked her to stay, but she wanted to help Piper with the baby, and I don't have many opportunities to get April alone, as I'm busy taking care of Hadley.

"We'll see about that." I tip her chin up with my finger, drawing her sight to me, and I'm tempted to press a warm kiss against her lips.

She seems to be onto me and tickles me away. "Down, boy. Go throw some balls or something. I need to get this frittata in the oven."

I still don't know how she manages to come up with a new recipe to cook every day.

"How about a swim before lunch?" I ask.

April gawks at me. "Do you literally fuck like a rabbit in the off-season to make up for baseball season when you keep it all in?"

I interlace our fingers, well, only with one of her hands, as the other is busy whisking. My need to keep her close unnerves me slightly, but I'm past the point of caring, this is what I want in this moment.

I'm already scolding her with my eyes as a grin tilts on the corner of my mouth. "It's not that I don't have sex during baseball season, I just don't do random hookups. If I'm in a relationship, then we work it out."

April bursts out laughing. "What in the world does that mean? Oh my God, you literally have a sex schedule around your games, huh?"

"That's maybe a stretch." Slightly. Barely.

"Good luck to her then." She returns to her experiment, and it causes me to pause that she doesn't see herself as a contender. It shouldn't bother me. A relationship is not what we are doing, but it feels close.

The sound of the door opening makes my head perk with attention to my mother walking in, carrying a laundry basket. She has the security code so she can come in when she wants, but she normally doesn't unless it's important.

"Oh, hey, sorry, I didn't realize you have company." My mother assesses the scene with intrigue as she slowly sets the basket on a chair at the kitchen island.

"It's fine."

I notice in the corner of my eye that April is straightening her apron as she watches my mother enter the picture.

"I guess you two only met briefly. Mom, this is April. April, my mom."

A genuine welcoming smile spreads on my mother's face. "Wonderful to meet you. Sorry, where are my manners." She stretches out her hand. "I'm looking at you so strangely, but I just thought you were staying for a few days."

April quickly wipes her hand on the apron before giving my mother a handshake hello. "Uhm, the plan kind of changed."

My mother's face immediately whips to my direction. "Fun."

I roll my eyes and clap my hands together. "What brings you by? How was the getaway?"

"Can't go wrong with Arizona. We're planning our next trip already. Your father wants to take me to Yellowstone so I can fulfill my Kevin Costner fantasy."

I shudder from the thought while April chortles a laugh and returns to her oven pan.

"I forgot I had all this laundry for Hadley. I was going to just leave it here and hoped to check if you lined up a babysitter for the coming period?"

My head drops slightly, and I rub my cheek while I groan. "The babysitter we had lined up dropped out due to a sick relative. I have my team reaching out to another agency to find someone."

My mom begins to look in her purse, probably for a Tic Tac if I know her well enough. "Spencer, it needs to get sorted out. Your father and I can't watch her forever. I love my grandbaby, and we will help when we can, but you know that it isn't what..." She pauses when she realizes she's struggling to finish the sentence.

I save her and jump in. "It's fine. I mean, I really just need someone to cook and clean, and I can take care of Hadley."

April offers me a soft reassuring smile before she turns to put her food in the oven.

"I'm happy to hear it, but you still need someone as a backup. Even in the off-season, you have all those fancy meetings, and you train a lot," my mother explains.

I sigh, as she makes valid points. "I'll find a way, okay." I'm getting slightly frustrated with this conversation; I don't enjoy being reminded of what I can improve on.

My mother turns her attention to April who doesn't notice, then returns her gaze to me. My mom's eyes grow big, as it is her way of asking for an explanation. I mouth back, *"Friend."* She subtly shakes her head that she doesn't believe me.

"I hope my son and his daughter aren't wearing you out," my mother says, attempting conversation.

"Not at all. Hadley is adorable," April comments.

"April has gotten Hadley to experiment with food," I add.

"Maybe you should be her next nanny then," my mother jokes.

April smiles. "I think you need a professional for that role, and I'm heading back to the city soon anyway."

Right, because April doesn't live here in Lake Spark unless I have a sex tape about to be leaked.

"Well, I'm going to leave you two alone. I have errands to

run. By the way, you remember Hadley has her check-up with the pediatrician next week, right?"

I salute my mother. "Yeah, it's in the shared calendar."

My mom waves to April and she says goodbye. A minute later, we are free from my mother's watch.

But still, I heave a sigh at the reminder of my responsibility. It makes me feel like everyone is waiting for me to fail when all I want to do is prove them wrong.

Leaning against the fridge, I wonder if this feeling of missing a piece will ever go away.

April nudges my arm with her own and comes to my side, and we both look forward at the ground. "She seems nice."

"Can't complain."

"Hadley will love having more time with you and less with a babysitter," she points out.

I'm not entirely convinced, and my face stiffens as I feel my lack of assurance set in.

April gives me a soft look, almost empathetic, as if she wants to say something more, but instead she smiles shyly and looks away before walking to the other side of the kitchen to grab Pickles' leash.

"Don't be in a grumpy mood today," she calls out. I'm bewildered as to how she understands my brain because I'm not exactly on the express train to happy right now. The last few minutes put a damper on my day.

Before I can argue, she is out of sight but not out of my mind.

Tiptoeing to Hadley's bed, I'm careful to lift the pillow under her head while she sleeps. Thankfully her night light is on, which gives me enough coverage to ensure my task is successful. Pickles perks his head up from where he is lying at the end of her bed.

Slipping the hundred-dollar bill under Hadley's pillow, I grab her little plastic treasure chest that holds a tooth.

I stroke her hair and take in the view of her lying there like a little angel holding a stuffed butterfly.

My journey out of her room is a slow walk, and I stop at her door to get one more image of her in my head, because every moment is another one gone, right? When I'm gently closing her door behind me, I'm startled.

"Tooth fairy duty?" April whispers as she leans against the wall in the hall, wearing her little shorts and tank. She must have been watching me this whole time, and I'm not sure how I feel about that.

I step to her, holding up the little treasure chest as proof. "First time."

"Oh yeah?" She arches a brow, and her fingers claw my shirt. "What's the going rate these days?"

"One hundred."

Her jaw drops, and she shrieks softly. "What? Are you crazy? Five would have sufficed."

I shrug. "Anything else you care to critique in relation to my tooth fairy skills?"

"Nah, but the tooth fairy is kind of hot." She pulls me closer.

Finally. We've been simmering in flirtation since we slept together. This is our moment to sizzle and pop.

An approving hum draws out of my throat. "No shit, the tooth fairy does it for you?"

"Uh-huh." This look on April is familiar. It's hungry, sultry, and playful.

Which is why I follow her as she tows me along to my room and walks me straight to the edge of my bed. Before I can process, I'm sitting and she's swinging a leg on either side of my waist to straddle me.

"This is not the role-playing scenario I had in mind," I joke.

"Nah, me neither. But watching you do the dad thing back there was… it does things to a woman." She drags her lips along my neck, and my dick is already hard.

I plant my hands on the sides of her body underneath the flimsy shirt. "What kind of things?"

"Dirty things. I would definitely go on the tooth fairy's bad list."

I snort a laugh, as this is slightly ridiculous, but I'm always a team player. "What in the world could you do to get on the bad list?"

"Use my tongue in inappropriate ways." She flashes her eyes at me.

I pull her flush against my body, and we fall back against the mattress. "I'm all game for a demo." Yet I wrap my arms around her and rub soothing circles on her back, keeping us in an embrace.

She peers up at me and studies me before she sighs a breath, but in a relaxing manner, not an annoyed way. April must pick up that I need a minute. I guess I'm having a delayed reaction to the fact that my little girl is having milestones.

"I… was wrong." She pops her lips.

"About what?"

"You are a great dad."

Looking down at her, I appreciate her words and the fact she genuinely means it.

"That's not what you said a week ago," I remind her.

"I was wrong."

My eyes grow wide. "Say that again."

"I... was wrong," she declares again.

I didn't realize that I needed this confidence boost, but it feels good. Sometimes, I feel like people around me are just waiting for me to fail. None of this was planned, after all.

The corner of my lip tugs, because I want to smile but don't want to appear that my ego is getting a boost.

Ah, what the hell.

"I think this tooth fairy deserves a reward," I mention.

April giggles as she adjusts her body and sits on top of me, wiggling her hips and creating friction against my cock before she slips down my body. She playfully brushes her lips along the waist of my jeans, tugging the button free, and her tongue hits the corner of her mouth in the process.

She peeks down into my boxer briefs before pulling them lower. The moment her lips wrap around my tip, my eyes instantly close from the feeling of her tongue gliding along my length.

I groan from the sensation. "You should go on every bad list of every fictitious character there is."

April pulls off for one second with swollen lips, her breathing labored. "I bet Santa has a whip." Then she's back on me.

I cradle her head between my hands, gently guiding her and holding her when she decides to take me deep.

Her eagerness only ups the ante, but it's watching her that is the true bonus of this moment.

"Right there," I breathe out as she finds the perfect movement.

This is going to be short-lived if I don't do something, but I want to be selfish. I'm allowed to be, I remind myself. Especially when I know I'll make it up to her another time.

And fuck me, because I'm already anticipating another

time. I don't think this is how we planned this whole situation to go.

She moans, and any logic exits my brain because she brings me back to the moment where there isn't a care in the world, just us having fun.

"April," I warn. "Be a good girl."

She understands and wraps her lips tighter around me. I swear I see colors in the air when I unload into her mouth, stroking her head as she works harder, and her eyes seek approval because that's who April is, a pleaser.

"You like that? Hmm? Taking every last drop?" I grit out as my climax overpowers me, especially when I feel her swallow.

With purpose, she slowly licks up my length until she circles my tip for good measure, creating space with a satisfied look. She walks her long fingers up my torso as I lie there, completely relaxed.

"There is no other way to do it," she rasps.

"You could leave me hanging."

She waves her finger in front of my face. "Ah-ah, I wouldn't dream of that since I have every intention of being repaid."

April begins to shift her way up my body with her knees on either side of me, straddling me.

"Why, whatever can I do to such a wicked girl?" I play along.

"You tell me. You are the one with magical powers tonight."

I feel my energy kickstart again, or it's the fact that I can feel she is ready for me where her pussy rests against my ribs.

A smirk possesses my lips. "Sit on my face, let me taste how much you're turned on from fucking me with your mouth."

She blushes but willingly moves until my head is trapped between her thighs, her pussy within a breath's distance, and I smell her sweet honey arousal. She glances down at me, maybe unsure or maybe to taunt me.

I kiss her inner thigh, tugging aside her skimpy sleep shorts to expose her core.

"Don't set yourself up for failure, sailor," she taunts, a phrase she said to me once on that very first night.

"Wouldn't dream of it," I promise. "Bite into your arm if you need to, we can't have you noisy, and I intend to eat you like a meal before my dick is buried deep inside of you."

Her eyes enlarge slightly and look impressed. "Don't go too crazy, I need to walk back to my room after this."

Her wet sweetness hits my lips before I can protest. Something inside me wants to say that she can stay the night and sneak out early.

Then again, fun is all we're doing. No?

18
APRIL

I watch through the window in the dance school between the waiting room and the studio. A little group of girls in leotards are dancing in a circle together. I can't help but smile at the little ballerinas who seem to be enjoying their class.

Spencer asked if I wanted to hang with him and Hadley, and it was an easy yes. He's in the car on the phone while I came in to pick up Hadley. He explained he doesn't enjoy listening to the dance moms who always have drama, so I would be doing him a favor; plus, his agent called in the car. Parents are only allowed to watch the kids dance during select weeks, but I can't help but be a rule-breaker.

"Sorry, are you here for Hadley?" the receptionist asks. She's sitting behind a little desk with a laptop. The woman herself looks like a dance teacher, my age too, and completely stunning, with light brown hair and a great complexion.

"Oh." I tuck a strand of hair behind my ear. "I am, actually."

"The new nanny?" She smiles politely.

"No, I'm..." Why can't I say a friend of Spencer's?

"Uhm, a friend of the family. Spencer asked me to help Hadley grab her jacket after class. He's out in the car."

She gives me the once-over, but her smile doesn't falter. "I get it." She tightens her ponytail. "I'm Romy, I own the studio."

"Oh right, well, this is a lovely little place. Hadley talks about dance class all the time." I do my best to be friendly.

"She is a sweet little girl." Romy holds a finger up. "Before I forget, her new ballet shoes came in." She leans down to a delivery box on the floor, filled with new shoe boxes, picks one up, examines the side to check the size, and then hands it to me.

"Thanks. I guess little feet grow fast," I comment.

Romy crosses her arms and looks at me, almost entertained. "I'm sorry. I must be staring, I just… I've never seen anyone here other than Spencer, his mom, or a babysitter that changes in rotation. I kind of thought Spencer doesn't really do relationships, you know?"

My brows arch, as I am trying to figure out if she is talking from experience or genuinely attempting to make conversation. "Really, it's nothing. We're good… friends."

"Good. Really good, perfect." Her lips roll in and then quirk out as she pulls her sweater tighter around her body, and I think I have my answer of why she is asking, but then she surprises me. "He doesn't let many people into his inner circle, but it's nice that he has, is what I mean."

"Sure." I nod.

The sound of the class wrapping up and a door opening from the studio breaks this awkward conversation.

"Well, maybe I will see you around. I've gotta run, I'm teaching the advanced pointe class next," she mentions and begins to move.

Advanced, of course.

Romy touches my arm in passing. "Please thank Spencer."

"For what?"

"I know it was him who paid for the extra shoes and costumes for one of my students whose family could use the extra help now." She offers me one more smile before heading off.

I don't have time to digest this fact that I've learned, as Hadley is skipping in my direction.

"April, did you watch me?" She hops in place with excitement.

"You bet I did. Those were some amazing sautés, mademoiselle." I place my hand on her shoulder and guide her to the wall of coats hanging on hooks to encourage her to gather her things.

Her bun nearly knocks me over when she leaps in front of me to grab her coat. "Where's my daddy?"

"In the car, but if we play our cards right then we can convince him to go to Jolly Joe's."

"Yes! I'm hungry."

"Well, then hot chocolate here we come." I tuck the box with her new shoes under my arm and follow Hadley to the front door. She waves to all her friends.

It's turning cold out, which means we race to the warm car. The moment we get in, I declare our plan. "The ballerina has spoken and to Jolly Joe's we shall go."

"Oh, has she?" Spencer gives me a knowing look.

"Please, oh please," Hadley pleads from the back with her hands together before petting Pickles who's sitting on the seat next to her.

Spencer rolls his eyes at me. "I'm outnumbered, aren't I?"

"You are." I toss the box to Spencer. "Here, her new ballet

shoes arrived. She should probably wear them around the house a little before she uses them, to avoid blisters."

"You're the pro, so I may actually listen to your advice." He begins to pull out of the parking spot, his forearms on display as he rests his arm on the back of my chair as he shoulder checks out the back window.

It's a few beats before I realize that Hadley is occupied with Pickles and this SUV is big enough that I can ask Spencer something I have no business knowing.

"You know who is a pro?" I begin. "I met the studio owner back there, a real delight, very interested in your private life."

Spencer gives me a humorous side glance before focusing on the road. "And?"

"I'm sure she is more than advanced at her techniques."

"Not having this conversation here," he rebukes.

I cross my arms and nearly huff, instead opting for silence for the next three minutes until we get to Main Street, and say nothing until we are inside Jolly Joe's and we order at the counter.

"Can I pick out a dog treat for Pickles?" Hadley asks before we sit down at a fifties-style booth. Jolly Joe's makes little peanut butter treats to give to dogs, as they are welcome here.

"Go wild," I say.

She skips off, and I check to make sure my loyal beagle is lying at my feet.

Spencer looks at me with a wry smile, and his eyes possess a curious glint.

"You were saying?"

He isn't going to let me forget.

I play with a napkin. "Nothing. Just all the dancers and

pioneers in this town over the age of twenty seem to be drawn to you, or is it you already went there with good old Romy?"

God, I hate the way I sound. Why do I care?

Spencer takes a sip from his water, calmy, almost as if he is calculating what to say. "I wouldn't hook up with someone who is responsible for Hadley's favorite hobby."

My nose tips up.

"I mean, that was the rule I made *after,* but you know," he adds. My mouth opens but no words come out until he starts to laugh. "Relax, I'm messing with you. Romy has a husband. She's high school sweethearts with the contractor for my house renovations, actually." My jaw relaxes, and I feel silly. Spencer reaches across the table to touch my arm. "Jealousy is kind of hot on you."

"I'm not jealous," I lie.

"A little jealous."

"Not at all."

"It's okay. I think I might strangle a guy who looks at you like he has a chance too."

My eyes dart to his, and I can't read him, but I sense that he is letting a chip off his steely exterior, and it causes a line to creep up on my mouth.

For a moment, I forget where we are, and it feels like it's only me and him, and I like that we are at peace with one another, relaxed enough to be ourselves with no walls, otherwise we will just tear them down. We aren't capable of hiding, not around each other.

"You know, many athletes perform good deeds and make a big thing about it for attention or publicity, but not you, Spencer Crews."

"What makes you say that?"

"Romy wanted me to thank you for the extra cash for supplies," I mention.

"Hmm. She must be confused." He avoids my penetrating gaze.

Admittedly, his lack of wanting praise is a surprise. This is the guy who loves to hear that he has a winning arm, but when it comes to a noble act he plays mute.

And that makes me add another point to the scoreboard when it comes to Spencer.

The waitress disrupts us when she brings us a giant kitchen sink of ice cream covered in whip cream, sprinkles, and a few cherries. Hadley is not far behind.

"This is dinner?" Spencer pretends to be unamused.

"No. This is what Hadley and I are eating for dinner. You were Mr. I Don't Eat Ice Cream So I Will Have a Water." I grab a spoon and scoot over so Hadley can sit next to me. "Don't forget our deal." I hand Hadley a spoon.

"I know. I have to eat some of the banana from the ice cream." She frowns.

"Banana splits are not banana splits unless you have a banana," I inform her again.

We both assess where to dig in first.

"Are you sure we can't convince you to have a bite? If you ask nicely, I'm sure we will share. Oh look, peanut butter, that's protein." I point out the section of the sink bowl with peanut butter and chocolate.

"Daddy doesn't eat many sweets. He's boring like that." Hadley speaks with a full mouth.

Spencer immediately looks taken aback. "Boring?"

"I'm sure he will prove us wrong." I hand him a spoon.

"He never eats ice cream," Hadley reminds me.

Spencer holds up his spoon for show before taking a spoonful of whipped cream and ice cream.

Hadley and I look on with interest and watch him eat his first bite. We both gasp at his move.

"I'm completely cool." He now speaks with his mouth full.

Hadley giggles before she takes another bite.

"See? I bet you want another bite too." I'm confident with my appraisal.

He tips his head in doubt, catching my eyes for a brief second, before ceremoniously dipping into the pile of ice cream again.

Hadley giggles, and this time a big smile erupts on Spencer's mouth. And the next twenty minutes is an abundance of ice cream tasting, smiles, and listening to Hadley talk ballet. I sense that it's their way of bonding, and I feel special that I get to witness it.

By the time we make it home, Hadley is out like a light, and Spencer carries her up the stairs. I follow because I just want to change into my pajamas, as the ice cream was heavy.

"April," Spencer loudly whispers.

"Yeah?" I yawn as we reach the top of the stairs.

Spencer turns to me, and it's quite a sight to see him holding a child this way. Another drop of my melting heart hits the ground.

"Want to sneak into my room in like an hour?" His voice does sound tempting.

"Hmm, maybe," I coyly reply and never confirm.

Instead, I walk straight to my room.

———

But, of course, I have no spine anymore around the man, so exactly sixty-two minutes later, I creep through the door to his bedroom to find him waiting in bed.

"You're late." He grins.

I stand before him and elongate my neck. "Ooh, were you counting down the seconds?"

He laughs and moves the duvet to invite me in. "Seconds is maybe a stretch, but I'll give you a minute or two."

I don't hesitate and slowly glide a few steps in the direction of the bed he has kept warm. "We keep meeting here."

Sliding between the sheets feels like a prize. It's all the things I enjoy; warmth, sex, and apparently, Spencer.

He lies on his side, quick to trace the lines of my body with his finger while he watches me sink against his mattress. "Why do I see a glimpse of something as pink as a Barbie?"

I laugh under my breath, as he must see my bra strap. I like my choice today; it's hot-pink and has strings across my cleavage. "Might have dressed for the occasion."

His mouth nips my shoulder as he sounds his endorsement. "I like the effort."

I reach up to stroke his face, my thumb rubbing a circle along his stubbled jaw. "Did you have a good day?"

"I did."

This is us having our moment. Where we check in with one another like two people who care and are attentive to one another before we go back to fulfilling each other's needs.

He combs his fingers into my hair. "I feel like I keep repeating myself and saying thank you a lot lately."

"It's called manners," I retort.

"Is it strange we just kind of gel together?"

"It happens when you live together, even if for a few days. But Hadley knows that I'm just a friend, right?" I double-check.

"I think so."

I draw a circle on his bare arm that is holding me. "I'll head back to the city at the end of the week, nonetheless. It's probably better for her."

He doesn't answer, but I feel his fingers entwine tighter around my locks.

"For now, I'll sneak out after you ravish me," I attempt to lighten the mood.

"Stay the night and sneak out in the morning," he states.

I peer up at him, and I see it's what he wants, maybe needs, but most of all, I hear a command, as if I'm his.

I nod in agreement before our lips meet for a kiss that I realize I've been craving since the last one.

Because I may not have figured him out, but he managed to peel away the layered walls that I had around him, and right now, I just want to fall asleep in the comfort of his arms after we do the one thing that we've always been good at; making each other feel free for a moment.

19

SPENCER

Opening my front door, I beam a smile when I find Hudson standing there with Gracie in a baby carrier on his chest, arms and legs stuck out like a starfish. In true Hudson fashion, he has sunglasses over his eyes and swipes them off with style, and a winning grin is permanent on his face.

The man is in his early forties but is the image of every man's hope of aging well, down to his lack of gray, not even a strand in his dark hair.

"I believe we need to discuss something," he announces.

I scratch my cheek and make an awkward attempt at a grin. "Don't you have a football team to coach?" I hold the door open as he walks right in.

My neighbor, friend, and April's uncle. I knew this moment would come, and somehow, I knew he wouldn't want to kill me either.

"I have a few hours off before I need to catch a flight for our next game, and I welcome the opportunity to investigate why I hear rumors around town that my niece is temporarily living with you, and my wife isn't spilling the tea."

"April isn't here, by the way."

"I know, I saw her leave with the dog for a walk. That's fine. I wanted to talk man to man." Hudson leans against the window wall of my living room.

I roll my eyes in entertainment. "April is heading back to the city, probably tomorrow."

"Why is she staying with you to begin with? I thought you two detest one another." It feels like his eyes are trying to catch me out.

I clear my throat. "She's using my kitchen."

His look tells me that he is waiting for more.

"Helping with Hadley."

Still no response.

"Can we leave it at that?" I try my luck.

He studies me for a second, looks down at his daughter, and his face softens. "Fine."

I blow out a breath of relief.

"Was it the baby shower?"

My eyes snap to him and panic sets in. "Baby shower?" My voice is uneasy.

"Yeah. I sent you back for a gift that I might not have really forgotten." He winks at me. "Was that the start of whatever you two young ones are up to?"

I chuckle a laugh. "You could say it's something like that." I kind of figured he was attempting a setup, but I gave him the benefit of the doubt.

"The thing is, I think this is great, you could use someone like her, and April deserves to move on from that little punk who I think we are all happy didn't lock her into marriage. But April is…"

"Feisty?"

"Yes, but I think she is still recovering a little from the last year. So, all I can say, and I know you know this, is that

April isn't one of those girls who will wait for you after your games for a good time. She can give a lot if that's what she receives. You'd be lucky."

I stare at him intensely, more because I'm lost in thought of her visiting me at a game.

"I hear what you are saying." Boy, do I hear him. He now has wheels turning in my head because I'm already trying to figure out what's happening.

"It's kind of big… I mean, she is involved with Hadley now."

"We're friends," I reiterate.

Hudson holds up his hand. "So you said." I hear the disbelief. "But I've never seen you bring any woman around Hadley that is just a friend."

I adjust my neck as he points out all the facts that I already know, and I'm well aware that anyone on the outside can see my predicament too.

"Uncle Bay!" April calls out as Pickles walks in before her. I forget she sometimes calls him a nickname, something about studying the Hudson Bay in school.

Hudson is quick to meet her halfway and offers an arm for a side hug. "Hey there. Heard you've been shaking up my neighborhood."

"Something like that." April gives him a hug and touches Gracie's head before walking into the kitchen. "Coffee anyone?"

"Sure. I have time for one quick cup," he calls out.

April is busy looking in a cupboard. "Hey, Spence, where are the extra coffee beans? They're in the pantry, right? Can you show me?"

"Ooh, she's calling you Spence," Hudson mumbles to me and flashes his eyes.

I laugh under my breath at this odd morning. "Be right

back."

Following April to the pantry, she's pretending to be searching for something before she closes the door behind us.

"He's here!" she loudly whispers. Her calm persona has faded into curious fear.

"Yeah, and? We knew he would eventually get the memo that you're shacking up in my humble abode."

"Is he being all… I don't know… uncle-y?"

"Is that a word?"

She pokes a finger into my chest. "Now isn't the time to be a smartass. I don't want him to find out what we did, I mean the video."

Now I'm having fun. "But he can know about everything else?"

She growls a sound before plunging forward to kiss me hard on the mouth. It is so fucking good. I like the way she kisses when it's spontaneous.

Pulling away, she smiles as her thumb glides along my jawline. "Thought you might need something to calm you down."

I step closer to her, framing her hips with my hands. "I'm calm. I don't falter under pressure. Babe, I'm a baseball player."

She bursts out laughing. "Well, won't you just save the world." She's mocking me. "Oh, look, I found the coffee!" she announces so Hudson can hear and reaches behind me to grab the coffee. I love that she follows through with her performance because I just filled the coffee machine this morning and I know it doesn't need beans.

Following her back into the kitchen with a bag of coffee beans, I know it's obvious that we look like two souls who just had a G-rated version of a frisky pantry fling. Proven by the fact that Hudson's smile is still just the way we left it.

"Heard you're heading back to the city," Hudson says to April as I lean over the kitchen island.

"Yeah, can't stay in this perfect little town forever." She focuses on pressing buttons on the coffee machine.

"You'll be back soon, I'm sure," he adds and then looks to his side at me.

"I mean, I always come visit Piper."

Why do I want her to say she'll come back for me and Hadley? This is Hudson's way to trigger my mind, I know his tactics.

April hands him a cup of coffee. "You know, I once had an uncle who was very adamant that I'm not allowed to date athletes. In fact, I wasn't even allowed to attend his games for fear a big bad athlete would hit on me. Where did that uncle go?" She feigns curiosity and brings her finger to her chin.

He grins wide at her humor. "Spencer isn't just an athlete, he's on my Hudson Arrows approved list. Besides, I need to focus on indoctrinating my daughter for the next eighteen years that athletes are a no-go, so I'm releasing you from my reins." His voice turns saccharine as he coos with his daughter.

"Don't be a player hater," April quips, and it causes me to laugh.

"Are we done with this topic?" I suggest.

Hudson waves a hand in the air. "Sure. I've made my voice heard." Hudson turns to me with his lips on the coffee cup, taking a sip. "By the way, Ford is going to come to one of my home games, want a seat also? A little neighborhood block party in the stands?"

"Sounds good."

"Swell. You'll be in the city then, and I'm assuming April is in the city too. Okay, great. That's me, gotta go." He strings words together, sets his cup down, and claps his hands.

I just shake my head at his ability to literally set us up for a last-minute play, no different than his football games when he coaches to win.

And maybe April could be the winning play in the home stretch.

———

April stands by her car and closes the door, with Pickles in the back.

"That's us, all packed and ready to go," she states.

She made a big breakfast for Hadley before coming with us for school drop-off. But her departure is happening now while Hadley is at school, which is probably easier.

I knock on the hood of her car. "Yep. Back to the city, free from me."

"Hmm, yeah."

She's trapped between the car and my body, and neither one of us seems ready to move. Last night we had dinner with Hadley, and after Hadley went to bed, April snuck into my room like she has been doing every night this week.

"I labeled a bunch of stuff in the freezer, in case you get stuck on dinner, since you don't have a babysitter yet," she mentions, and I love that she's taking care of us as a parting gift.

"We'll eat it, I'm sure," I promise.

Her eyes are searching for a clue.

"You'll let me know when you get back? Those foxes on the road, you know. They come out of nowhere."

Her closed lips move side to side. "Just like pitchers, I guess."

"Why is that plural?" I raise a brow.

She grabs hold of my open jacket. "Pitcher. He was a real piece of work at the start."

I slant a shoulder up to my ear. "Bet you loved it."

She nods once.

We are drawing out this minute. "It's been fun." She looks away, and I can tell she's putting up a defense.

But I want to tear it down.

"April."

Her eyes meet my own, hopeful. "Yeah?"

"Do you think that I can visit you in the city?"

"Sure. You're always welcome." She doesn't seem to get it.

I tilt her chin up with my long finger. "As in, I want to keep seeing you. I can visit you, and you can visit us here."

A smile begins to form. "I mean, I guess that makes sense. Pickles and Hadley kind of have a bond I'm jealous of."

I step closer, bringing her mouth closer to mine, at a distance that has our breaths mingling. "Stop avoiding the obvious. You don't want this to stop, and I don't want it to either."

"Telling me what I feel, now?" She's impossible, yet I grin before I slam my lips onto hers to kiss her and to confirm that I'm absolutely right.

She dips her tongue into my mouth to deepen our kiss. A sound vibrates from the back of her throat into my mouth as her body arches into mine.

I don't dare break this moment, but we can't stay like this all day. But damn, there is a fire inside of me that I didn't know was possible. A want for someone that I can only describe as new, but I'm not ready to let it go.

She reluctantly breaks away; our lips push and pull in a magnetic dance.

"You're right," she rasps between kisses.

"I'm always right."

I cradle her face in my hands and our eyes lock. I even nuzzle our noses together, and I'm beginning to wonder what version of myself this is, softer for sure, and I recognize a sweltering flare inside of me that realizes this woman could bring me to my knees because I want her.

"I guess I'll be seeing you around then?" She attempts to hide her smirk.

"Lucky you." I follow her to the driver's seat and hold the door open as she slides into her seat.

"Yeah, maybe I am," she laments.

I hope she is because that would mean I'm the guy that deserves to share a life with someone like her, and I'm still not sure I believe that.

20
APRIL

Folding laundry is a boring Sunday task, but I light a beeswax candle, clean the apartment, and use the day as a reset for the week. I've also been listening to my mother for the last ten minutes debate if the sweater she bought me is forest green or palm green, whatever the hell the difference is.

"I can return it if you want. But it does look great on you, fits perfectly, and most importantly, will keep you nice and warm for winter." She folds the sweater and slides it to the other side of the counter before grabbing her mug of coffee.

"It's fine." I focus on folding my laundry. Pickles is crashed out on the couch.

My mom and I went for brunch, and after, she came back to my apartment, because I know she likes to check everything is in order because I'm forever her baby. I live in a simple apartment, but it's in a safe building with a condominium board that ensures the elevator always works.

"I guess staying warm is already taken care of for the winter," she mumbles before pretending to take a sip of her coffee.

I stop folding and look at her with a jarring stare. "Something you wish to bring up, dear mother?"

She smiles warmly. "You were looking at your phone all the time when we were at the restaurant."

"And? It's how people these days transfer messages, share updates on their life, send inappropriate GIFS." I find a missing sock and pair it together. I know where she is going with this, and Spencer and I have been messaging all week. Updates about Pickles, Hadley, his questions about reheating food I left, and jokes that I'm sure he heard in the locker room.

"I know, I get your bombardment of Pickles photos, and the Arrows family group chat is a delight during football season," she jokes. "But I have a feeling a particular baseball player is responsible for keeping you distracted. You didn't even steal a bite of my cheesecake today."

Throwing the sock pair into the laundry basket to put away later, I glance at my mom and debate what to say. "Your point?"

"You haven't really updated me on what's going on with your romantic life, maybe even avoided that topic, and I didn't want to push. *However*, the radiant smile that doesn't leave your face has me interested, and I'm going to assume Spencer is the culprit since you had a little getaway to Lake Spark."

I bite my lip before my defense completely falters. "Can I plead the fifth?"

"Not with me."

"Fine. Yes, he *may* be responsible for my mood." Now I can't help but gush, and I feel my facial expression give me away.

My mom taps her nails on her mug. "Do tell."

"We... are... just going with the flow, you know how it

is." I wave a hand at her, and she gives me the warning glare that she needs more data. "Early stages. Just seeing where it goes. No rush. No need for nosy mothers to get involved."

"Good. Enjoy it, and the moment you think your mother who is a smart cookie needs to be involved, then you phone me."

I nod and grab my own mug of tea. "You know, for someone who is excellent at tearing down the opposition in a courtroom... did you not see the signs with Jeff?" It's funny how once a relationship ends, everyone states how they were never in favor of it. Could have used the clue beforehand.

My mother grabs her purse and walks to me, tentatively touching my arm. "When you think you're in love, you choose to see what you want. Would you have listened? Besides, you're my daughter, so I'm blind when it comes to you. I wanted you to be happy, and maybe that's what I tried to see, even if I had doubts. But you are a strong lady who will end up with someone better. All exes lead to the one."

"Let me guess, you're hoping it's a star pitcher?"

She bobs her head side to side. "He isn't half bad." Her smirk tells me enough; she approves.

I offer a half-smile before she hugs me goodbye.

The next hour, I finish up the laundry, unload the dishwasher, and take a long shower to unwind for the rest of the day. A long binge session of *The Bear* is calling my name.

But as I'm about to hit the play button, I hear a knock on my door, which is strange, as the doorman would normally call up. Pickles decides that he needs to act the part and actually jumps off the couch and attempts to run to the door.

Following, I glance down to ensure I'm halfway decent. I'm in Piper's original pajama bottoms and a tank that stops at my midriff. Meh, it will have to do. I wrap my cardigan tighter around my body.

Opening the door, excitement hits me in a wave, but I play it cool because Spencer is standing on the other side of the door, leaning against the frame with a faint grin on his lips. His coat is open to reveal his jeans and dark fitted sweater.

"Surprise," he informs me with a piercing gaze.

My hands find my hips. "Indeed, a shock." My voice remains calm and even.

"Aren't you going to invite me in?"

"For the guy who probably paid off the doorman and then showed up while I'm in my pajamas?"

He takes a step forward through the doorway, ignoring my feigned attempt to prolong our front-door conversation. "I don't think I've ever complained about your pajamas before, so no issue." Spencer walks into my apartment, looking around curiously. He drops a small overnight bag to the ground.

Pickles' tail wags as he remembers Spencer. He sniffs once then returns to the living room.

Closing the door lazily behind me, I scoff a sound of utter amazement as Spencer confidently walks in as if he owns the place. It's not even arrogance, it's a swagger that I've learned is a natural part of his personality.

"You know it's rude to invite yourself in."

He takes hold of my hands, interlaces our fingers, and gives me a tug in his direction. "I'm sure you would have."

"What brings you by?" We didn't have it on the calendar to see one another again until next weekend. I was going to drive up to Lake Spark because it's just easier with Hadley.

"My publicist needed to reschedule a meeting for tomorrow morning, so I thought I would surprise you."

My lips curl into a smile. "Guess I'll have to cancel my Sunday-night date."

"Funny." He pulls me tight to his body. "If you don't mind, I'll be crashing here tonight."

I tip my chin up. "Oh, will you now?"

Spencer growls as he plants his lips on mine to kiss me hello. It's soft but by no means weak. Pulling away, he touches the tips of our noses. He's being... sweet.

"Where's Hadley?" Finding a babysitter hasn't been easy.

"My mom is watching her and taking her to school tomorrow."

I loop my arms around his middle. "I see. We'll have to order in for dinner; I'm not in the mood to cook."

His eyes haven't left me. "Sounds good. We'll order later from that new Italian place. They don't deliver, but they owe me a favor."

"I might kind of like you because of that. Later? We have other plans first?"

Spencer chuckles and slides my cardigan off one shoulder, dragging the strap of the tank top and bra down to reveal bare skin. He kisses me on the curve then trails a line of kisses up to my neck. "It's my first time here, but I think I have an idea of where we need to go."

In one swift move, he lifts me up and throws me over his shoulder, fireman style. I squeak and squeal as he carries me to my bedroom.

Throwing me onto my mattress, he moves over me with a sly grin, and I can't wait. My lips search for his, and I kiss him.

Then I urge him to roll over, taking me with him. Our lips tease, and we smile against one another's skin.

"I think you're happy with my unexpected appearance," he rasps, kissing my jawline.

"Don't put this on me. You're the one who probably missed me because I'm amazing," I counter.

He rolls me back so that I'm under him again. "Don't get cocky now."

"No, that would be your hard dick that's pressing into me."

His head falls forward near the corner of my neck as he laughs.

And for a moment we stop in our frantic moves to stay in an entranced gaze before he places a long deep kiss against my lips, and I wrap my legs around his waist.

Swallowing, I'm scared to blink and to find this could be a dream.

"You're right. I'm not complaining that you're here," I whisper. "Shh. Don't you dare come out with an arrogant remark and ruin the moment," I warn.

A devilish smirk forms on his mouth. "Wouldn't dream of it. Now let me inside before I lose my mind." His hand disappears between us, and my body follows his lead.

And to my surprise, we move slowly, savoring the moments as clothes disappear and our hands explore. The moment he's inside of me, I now know another fact about Spencer Crews; he's trouble for my emotional state.

Lying in bed with my head against Spencer's chest, the sheet is tangled around us. His fingers graze my arm in long strokes.

"Can I ask you something?" I break our silence as we've laid quietly for a few minutes.

"Sure."

"I know you use my mom's firm for your legal stuff. Hope you get a neighbor discount since Hudson is her brother, but like, how much have you worked with my mom?

She's not allowed to say, yet she seems to be a fan and not in the baseball sense."

He scoffs a laugh and squeezes me tighter. "Enough. She helped with some family law matters. You two have a few similarities, but you are quite different too."

"I would say I get that from my father, but I don't know who that is."

Spencer dips his gaze down. "It's not about biology when it comes to being a parent." His tone is firm, adamant almost.

"I know, but my curiosity runs deep."

"Ever thought of running one of those genealogy test kit things?"

I think for a second. "No. I guess I don't want to rock the boat, you know? I was given a great life, and in the end, it was a choice of whomever it was and a choice for my mom to have me this way. He gave her a gift, so that's enough for me to respect his decision, whomever he may be."

Spencer seems to ponder my words. "I wonder if more people have that theory," he states simply. "Do you think you are at peace with it all because you always knew? Like, what would you have done if you found out when you were older?"

"I think knowing from the start is a big part, but everyone is different. I had a friend who was adopted and only found out when she was eighteen, and it got to her. She wished she never knew, because her parents were her parents, and their lack of shared genes wasn't an important fact that she needed to know. I guess they are all okay now, though."

"Right." He goes quiet for a second. "Can I ask you something now?"

"Of course."

"You want kids one day?"

His question surprises me. "Wow, we are already at this stage of discussion?" I tease him, and he flashes me an unimpressed look. "It's not something I have an overpowering feeling about, but I think one day, yeah. If you are asking if Hadley is an issue, then, well, you know I like her more than you."

Spencer smiles to himself and begins to brush my hair with his fingers.

"She doesn't know that I'm seeing you. I just told her I had a meeting in the city."

"I get it. We don't really know what we're doing. My mom never introduced any dates until they hit the three-month mark, there were only a few."

"I think we know what we're doing."

The tips of my fingers land on his cheek to guide his head in my direction. "Do share."

"If I needed a fuck-buddy then I have options."

My mouth goes slack. "Wow, you better speed up your explanation."

His other hand holds my arm in place because he probably knows I want to swat him with it.

"I'm just saying that you're not that, and you know more about me than most. I would like to think next time you visit Lake Spark I don't need to sneak you in and out of my room. And when baseball season hits, then you'll be there in the stands."

He just did a one-eighty because that's the total opposite to where I thought this conversation was going. "Baseball season is still a few months away," I point out.

"Then tell me what timeline you're working with."

"I don't have one. I just… not getting hurt is more my priority. The last year has been one letdown after another from the men in my life. It takes a little to recover."

"I get that."

I focus on the tattoo on his skin. "Will you get another one?"

"Probably."

"Hey, since we're asking questions, out of curiosity, what would your girlfriend do during baseball season other than fuck on a schedule?"

"Come to my games. I don't know, haven't had one in a while." He kisses along my collarbone.

"Girlfriends are hard to come by, I hear." I pretend to be unaffected that all his words and moves today are making me giddy inside.

"I do have high criteria. Cooking is a plus." He kisses lower. "Sparkly powder on their skin that highlights their curves is a bonus." And lower. "A mouth that I want to kiss sometimes to shut her up is damn near the perfect find."

"Hmm, sounds like you might have found someone." I close my eyes and my breath feels calm.

Spencer kisses the valley between my breasts. "I think I have. She just needs to step up to the home plate when she's ready, because I think I am."

My chest thumps like my heart wants to break free. "Hmm, is that what that white square thing is? I'm there. Just need to see if we are the winning team together."

He moves to my belly button, stationing himself between my legs as he lies on his stomach. "I'll take the challenge."

His tongue hits the perfect spot, but it's the honesty so apparent in his eyes that sends a chill down my spine.

21

SPENCER

I stare at the box that April just tossed onto my sofa. I'm not sure what this stuff is.

The other week, I got overcome with a need to see her, and I surprised her at her apartment. Eating takeout while being forced to watch a new series was kind of a relaxing change. The next morning, April grabbed breakfast when she walked Pickles and brought it back so we could avoid running into people. She didn't let me forget that fact, as she teased me several times, but I prefer staying under the radar when I'm in the city.

I only barely managed to leave her place, because I knew she would be back to Lake Spark, and I had my agent waiting for me.

April drove up and arrived a few minutes ago. I'm still in my workout gear and am kind of sweaty since I hit my gym for an extra session, as Hadley is with a friend at her house after school.

"That's everything," April announces and collapses on the couch next to me and places her feet on the coffee table.

"Explain."

She giggles and rolls her head to the side to look at me. "Relax, I'm not moving in. I just have a few extras for this visit."

"Oh yeah?" I begin to rummage through the box. I pull out a new makeup kit, but it appears to be for a child. "Hell no."

"It's fine. It's not real makeup. It goes on clear against the skin."

"What's the point then?" I toss it back into the box.

April's mouth opens and pretends shock. "Make-believe, silly."

I roll my eyes, even though I know Hadley will be over the moon. "The only make-believe I'm going for is a little role-play between us."

She snickers a laugh. "Oh yeah? What did you have in mind?"

I don't really have anything in particular in my head, I just said it in jest.

"Look in the box," she demands.

Searching the box, I notice a fancy square with a bow. Grabbing it, I hold it up to check this is what she meant, and she nods.

"Know what it is?" she asks and seems like she's trying to contain her excitement.

I study the label. "It's from Piper's boutique."

"Uh-huh." She brings her knees to her chest and bites her lip, patiently waiting for me to get a clue.

But I'm confused. "You got another pair of fruit-print pajamas?"

She nearly scorns me with her look. "Get there faster," she urges. "Piper also has another line of evening attire." She raises her brows and waits for me.

Got it.

"*Really?*" I'm fully invested now and tug the bow.

"Yep."

Lifting the lid off the box, I'm faced with a layer of tissue paper. "Isn't it weird to buy lingerie from your aunt?" I taunt her because I know she hates being reminded that her best friend became her aunt.

"I'm regretting my effort, right now."

Searching through the paper, I feel lace. An approving growl escapes my mouth as I hold up the thin strings of black lace to reveal a one-piece with little triangles that will barely leave much to the imagination around April's breasts, and quite frankly, this see-through lace may be an obstacle to reaching the real treasure.

"Fuck me, I don't regret your effort one bit." I lean across the couch to capture her mouth for a kiss, and she circles her arms around my neck. She pulls me to her, and I fall on top of her which causes her to giggle. "I'm all sweaty," I say, with our lips still attached.

"I like you sweaty," she says huskily.

"I should go shower, and you can meet me upstairs. We have a window of opportunity."

April pulls back and waves her finger in front of my face. "Uh-uh, Mr. Eager, I need to get dinner started."

"It's not even three o'clock." My voice breaks.

She hops off the couch and straightens her shirt. "I know, but I want my soup to simmer, and I need to send my resume to a few job opportunities that I saw online."

"I want to simmer. Inside of you." I hear my lack of enthusiasm, even though she's attempting to put a damn good meal on the table later.

April makes a sound and sends a flirty glare my way before leaving me with a hard-on and impatience.

I rest my head against the back of the couch and close my

eyes. I attempt to breathe some calmness into my body, but no luck.

"Spencer!" She sounds kind of pissed now. It causes me to get up off the couch and look to the kitchen where she has her hand over her mouth and seems like she might combust.

"What now?" I walk to her.

"Are you kidding me?" Her eyes narrow in on me as I approach her.

I hesitate, as I'm not sure what's going on. "With what?" Her arm splays out to the direction of the mixer. "Uhm, it's a mixer."

"It's not just a mixer. This wasn't here last time."

"And?"

"It's the one I mentioned once. It has like a gazillion different functions." She walks to the red machine and begins to assess all the little features.

I might have ordered it with her in mind. It's huge so will never fit in her kitchen, which makes me internally question why buying her supplies for my kitchen is coming so naturally. But I wanted to do something for her. We're past flirtation, and we could be something longstanding. I've mentioned my intentions, but that doesn't mean we need to make a big deal out of my gestures, though I'm sure my mother would call it sweet.

"No biggie." I downplay this act because I need to. I can't overthink this.

She slowly walks to me, step by step, ensuring our eyes hold, giving me a chance to stare at her soft lips stretching into a smile. "Now I'm going to have to replan the entire weekend menu," she chides.

"My fault?"

She nods. "You never make it easy for me."

"It's no fun that way." I welcome her into my arms. I miss having her in my kitchen daily. "Plus, I'm not a good guy."

"So I thought," she faintly replies, and it feels sentimental.

Her fingers claw my shirt, and I know her well enough now to know that she wants to ditch her kitchen plan and instead head upstairs, which I'm on board with.

"Going to join me in the shower or wait for me in bed?"

"Join you in the shower, for sure," April purrs.

I lift her up at the same time she climbs me like a tree. We make it to the bottom of the stairs, but my phone goes off, and as much I hate to break the mood, it could be the mom who is letting Hadley play with her daughter.

"Babe, I need to check."

She's already reaching into my pocket with her hand, which causes her to feel my cock through my pants, but I'm sure that's what she wanted. She pulls out my phone and wiggles it in the air with pride.

I read the screen and see the message that Hadley will be dropped off soon, as they're on the way back from the park.

Humorously, I laugh to myself because this is our luck. "We have ten minutes tops."

"Doable," she promises.

"That's my girl." I continue us on our path upstairs, very much aware that April may just be my girl.

LOOKING INTO HADLEY'S ROOM, I see she isn't in her bed as promised, to wait for her bedtime story. Somehow April managed to get Hadley to eat tomato soup with grilled cheese that she cut into shapes, then we watched a Christmas movie. But it's way past Hadley's bedtime now.

Walking down the hall to the guest room, I spot the door open and hear Hadley.

"Why are you sleeping in here?" she asks, and I hear April crack a sound.

"Uh, why wouldn't I?" April has doubt in her tone.

"Nova, my friend, said that you are a special friend of daddy's. It's what her daddy has too, because her parents don't live together, so she has two houses."

Clearing my throat, I swoop right into the room to end this conversation. "There you are, sweet pea, I thought I said wait in bed."

"But I wanted to say good night to April," she justifies and looks up at me so innocently.

"That's sweet of you, but it looks like April could use some alone time."

April shoots me a humorous stare. "April can speak for herself, and it's fine."

"I kind of figured you are a special friend of daddy's."

I rub the back of my head and debate what to say. "Is that a problem?"

"No." Hadley seems unfazed and unconcerned. "But Nova said special friends sleep in daddies' rooms, so why is April staying here?"

April sets her brush on the bed and kneels down to Hadley. "Because I was just a friend of your dad's, and just friends stay in the guest room."

And I'm tapping in.

"But now she is a special friend, so it will change. I'm sure April was just visiting this room for old times' sake." This is our opportunity to smooth the sails and make the transition, plus I want to be a selfish man tonight. Something inside of me wants to dive in, but that's always the case when April is around.

"Or April is in here because we didn't agree on the timeline for this conversation," April mumbles to me.

I touch Hadley's shoulder. "Are you okay with all of this, sweet pea?"

She looks between us. "Am I ever! I get a dog."

"Well, you don't exactly get Pick—" April cracks out an attempt.

I'm quick to intercept with a smile. "Pickles is yours most of the time." We have to keep this convo smooth.

April gives me a comical warning glare because I shouldn't be throwing out false promises.

"Nova also said that there are special friends and there are girlfriends. Which are you?" she asks April.

"Nova's father has been busy," April tells me, and I have to agree. She returns her focus to Hadley. "I'm…"

April looks to me for a clue, and I answer for us. "April is more than a special friend, a lot more." I'm not going to put her any peg lower because she *is* more; she makes me happy and fits into our life.

"Like she will be my new mommy?"

Fuck, an arrow through my heart. I knew this would come up, how can it not when you're a child? It's just a harsh reminder that I need to tread carefully because I have the ability to break both of these ladies' hearts if I don't approach our dynamic with care.

In this moment, I have no words because my head is spinning at the reminder that Hadley doesn't have a mom, and I feel my mood sink. Not for any reason April would guess.

"Wow, aren't we full of questions today," April says. "You know, getting a mommy is a big deal. It requires a lot of time and sparkly powder before you can welcome a mommy into your life. Even if we enjoy being around someone, we have to wait before we can welcome them into our life that way. I had the exact same experience as you when my mommy found someone."

"Okay, I'll ask again later."

"Like a few months later," April suggests before tapping Hadley's nose. "Now I think it's way past your bedtime. Is Pickles already waiting?"

"Yep. Will you help me tuck him in?"

April stands and offers her hand to Hadley. "Always." She gives me a reassuring half-smile.

Lucky for me, April answers with the type of care that makes me wonder if long-run us isn't so crazy.

———

STANDING in the middle of my bedroom, I stare at April who is standing in the doorway giving me a curious smile.

"You're not in bed?" she wonders and steps into the room.

Truthfully, I'm too anxious to settle under the covers. I'm a smart man to know that it's because of what just went down half an hour ago with Hadley. Maybe I'm slightly shaken.

"You okay? You were a little quiet during the bedtime routine."

I lunge forward and cup her face in my hands before crashing my mouth onto hers. "Can we not talk?" I plead.

She studies my eyes for a moment and seems to grasp that I need an escape and she nods gently.

Kissing her again, I lead her back to the door and pin her arms up.

"No bed?" she muses in a whisper.

My answer is to lift her up and walk us a few steps and plant her on the dresser, causing something to fall to the floor, but neither one of us cares.

"Okay, no bed," she answers her own question before kissing me again.

I grip both sides of her flimsy t-shirt, and in one pull, I tear the fabric open, and my mouth travels her skin with no ordered pattern. I just want to take what she is offering. She doesn't question it either as her hands help lower my shorts, and it doesn't take long before I'm pounding into her, as she is ready and willing.

Her legs tremble and her pussy squeezes. My mouth seems to be taking my inner wrath out on her. The dresser shakes, and her breathy moan breaks my delirious thought.

I place my hand against her mouth. "Shh, baby, we have to be quiet. You understand?" I whisper, and she nods, with her hair now a disheveled mess. Removing my hand, I can't stop staring at her swollen lips. "Squeeze more," I demand.

Her eyes try to pry an answer out of me as to where my mind is, but I offer no answer because her body follows my cues, and her arms hold me tighter.

"Spencer," she whispers.

"Am I hurting you?" My voice is hoarse.

"No. Deeper."

I groan into her ear, because that's my girl, joining in on this ride.

We stay a tangled mess on top of my dresser until we both come undone sooner than I would have hoped.

She rubs circles on my back, as I stay put inside of her. I appreciate that she doesn't ask what just happened, because the truth is that she has managed to sneak into my life to the point that I don't ever want her to go, but my body and brain have connected that this means I need to share the secrets that I've been holding onto and may just push her away…

22

APRIL

Brushing Hadley's hair, she is wiggly today.

"Two more seconds then we're done, I promise." I touch her shoulders to force her to look straight. She has on her favorite dress, because today is a special occasion.

"What's going on?" Spencer asks as he enters the living room.

I quickly glance over my shoulder, trying not to lose focus on my task. "We're getting ready."

"For what?"

Closing the clip in Hadley's hair, I scoot her away. "All done. Just don't get messy." Turning my full attention to Spencer, I plaster on a big smile. "I have a surprise."

He scratches the back of his neck, unsure. "What would that be?" He peers over my shoulder and notices a woman with dark hair outside. "Who is that?"

Stepping closer to him, I take his hands in mine. "Don't kill me, but I know someone who takes pictures, and I think your walls could use some family photos. You don't really have many."

"Oh." His look is perplexed. "I guess, you did mention once that I keep the house compartmentalized."

Tugging him with me, we walk to the living room wall where there are photos. It's just Spencer and baseball teams. The only somewhat personal one is of him in which he looks like he is in high school with a friend. They seem to be laughing in the parking lot next to a baseball field, I can tell by the fence in the background.

"Sport photos make sense, but a few photos of you and Hadley will make this wall perfect, don't you think?" I ask, noticing his eyes are stuck on the photo from high school.

He swallows a breath. "Yeah." His voice is supple.

I stand on my toes to kiss his cheek. "I booked a photo session for you and Hadley. You will have a bunch of photos to choose from."

His face softens, and a smile forms. "That's really sweet of you."

"Is it? You look not convinced."

His smile turns sincere. "I just never thought to do something like this. But it's really… special. Thank you."

He leans down to kiss my mouth.

"Just throw on some nice jeans and a sweater. You don't need to match."

"It's not like matching pajamas or some shit like that?"

I shake my head. "No. I promise, you won't even know the photographer is there. Super natural and just be yourselves."

Spencer looks at Hadley who is staring out the window at the photographer while she tests her camera, then his eyes return to me.

"I don't know what to say."

I quirk my lips out. "Nothing. The thing about relationships is we get to surprise one another."

He pulls me tightly to his body to hug me tight, lifting me off the ground slightly. "You're right. Okay, let me go change."

A quick peck on my lips and he sets me down before going upstairs. I touch my heart, knowing this will be a wonderful day for Spencer and Hadley, which is exactly what I wanted for them. It selfishly makes me happy to be able to do something for them; that's what caring for someone and love are, right?

STROLLING SLOWLY BEHIND THE PHOTOGRAPHER, I do my best to stay out of the way. My cheeks hurt from smiling so much.

In this moment, Spencer is down on one knee on his dock with Hadley sitting on his bent leg. He's showing her a baseball, and I think because Hadley loves the camera experience, she's taking an interest. I can't hear what he is saying to her, but it makes her giggle.

During the last hour, we've tried different poses in various locations outside. Even though it's chilly, they are dressed warmly enough. This scene, however, seems to be the winning shot.

"April," Spencer calls out.

He indicates for me to join him, but I shake my head. This is their time. He ignores me and still persists.

The photographer glances at me. "Go on."

I'm still reluctant, but now Hadley is waving for me to join them too. Hesitating, I walk over.

Spencer stands, with Hadley by his side, staring at me with a smile. The feeling of Spencer's arm pulling me close causes me to smile.

"You know, there is an unwritten rule that unless you're

married or the baby momma or daddy, one should not ruin family photos. You never know if you have to erase someone out," I joke.

"I will gladly take the chance." He pulls me tighter, and my body curves into his shape. "Besides, it's just a few."

I squeal when he kisses my neck, and a tickle races down my spine.

"Thank you," he whispers.

"Having fun?" I ask both of them.

"Yeah," Hadley answers before running off to Pickles who is trailing behind the photographer.

The photographer follows Hadley to grab a few photos with her and Pickles.

"Pickles didn't get the memo about the unwritten rule," I comment as I watch them.

"Relax," Spencer assures me.

My eyes meet his gaze. "You have some great photos. You're such a natural in front of the camera, Hadley too. She must get that from you."

"It must run in our blood."

His lips twitch for a second, but whatever thought is in his mind, he ignores it as he tips me back for a deep kiss. Clearly, my surprise was a success.

———

Sitting on the sofa, we just put Hadley to bed and are ready to look at a few unedited photos that the photographer sent.

"She is fucking adorable," Spencer proudly states as he sees the first photo where Hadley is hanging off the branch of a tree.

"Boys will go wild for her when she's older."

"Not on my watch," he warns while he slides his thumb across the screen.

"You can pick a few to blow up and frame. The rest we can make into a photo book. You must have a photo book of Hadley somewhere from when she was a baby."

Spencer doesn't look up. "Somewhere. I love this one." He holds the phone up to display the photo of him showing her the baseball while they were on the dock.

"Thought you would."

"My mom will go crazy for this."

"We'll make sure they get a copy."

We both pause when we see a photo of just the two of us. It almost scares me how natural and happy we look.

"Not bad."

He gives me a pointed look. "This is a keeper."

I don't say anything, instead watch him swipe to the last photo and nearly gasp. It's all three of us, and I have butterflies in my stomach. It's confronting, but in a good way. My eyes land on a perfect photo of a family of three. Three people who seem immensely happy. It fills my soul with hope.

"A good memory," he notes as his thumb traces the screen.

"A keeper," I repeat his words from before.

But I don't want us to get too sentimental. Maybe we should slow down, but I don't want to. I should, considering my history, but everything feels so right.

I bounce off the couch because a million thoughts are floating in my head. Walking to the wall of baseball photos again, I cross my arms.

Spencer is fast behind me, his arms wrapping around me from behind.

"You okay?"

"Totally," I lie.

He kisses my cheek as we both look forward, yet neither one of us seems to be looking at anything in particular. "Thank you for today. It was unexpected yet exactly what we needed. Sometimes I forget that a photo can be the proof. I actually look like a good father in the photos."

"You shouldn't have doubts." But he does, I sense it sometimes. He is confident about everything, except slightly shaky when it comes to his daughter.

We stand there in an embrace for a good minute, just holding one another.

"High school you was kind of hot," I say, breaking the ice, my head indicating to the photo.

"Thanks. Some people would say I had it all from the start, but I'm beginning to think I'm only just realizing what that means."

His words strike me, I can't pinpoint why, but when I look over my shoulder, I can see that Spencer seems lost in thought again.

And any worry I have, I do my best to bury.

23
APRIL

I interlace my arm with Piper's as we watch through the window the ice hockey game down below. We are in the box seats, which means we have an abundance of snack options behind us.

"It's nice that you got away for a night," I mention. The baby is nowhere in sight.

"Much needed. The joys of having an adult stepson. It means he can do babysitting duty with his wife. My grandmother is great, but she can't handle overnight visits. Anyways, Hudson and I put Lucy and Drew up in a fancy hotel room with the promise they will watch Gracie for a few hours. Tomorrow I will take her to visit my grandmother before stopping by the football field to see our favorite coach," she explains while her head angles as she tries to follow the game happening.

"I'm still upset you didn't bring the baby," my mother calls out from where she stands next to the buffet because her law firm supports the team.

I take a sip of my beer bottle and ignore her. "Remind me

again why every athlete in Lake Spark decided to use my mother's firm for their legal woes."

Piper smiles and touches my shoulder. "Because they follow Hudson's advice when they need a city lawyer who is a shark in heels. Plus, I am super confident they get a discount."

"Fun." I'm not enthralled.

We both search for our men. Ford invited us all to watch his hockey game since they are now heading into mid-season and, according to him, are now in their prime of excellence. Spencer and Hudson went to sit down by the ice where there is more action, and I think they did it for a media op to show support for Ford.

"I bet Ford's ex is here somewhere," Piper notes.

"She comes to games?"

"Yeah, more for their son than anything is my guess. They are on good terms, just not the terms Ford probably wants. I've met her a few times, and Brielle is super sweet. She's studying law and interns at your mom's firm. Brielle doesn't like coming to Lake Spark, but maybe we should invite her to something here in the city."

"Why not? Is there some secret athlete partner's club that I get initiated into?" I try to keep my smile small.

Piper nudges my shoulder. "It would seem like you and Spencer are on a path forward."

"Surprisingly so." But as much as he has been the kind of boyfriend a girl could dream of the last few weeks, especially since Hadley discovered our secret, not to mention he makes my heart flutter and occupies my thoughts, I can tell something is on his mind. "I just hope he doesn't get cold feet. That tends to happen when men are around me."

"You think that's happening?"

I shrug a shoulder and then my face squinches. "Yikes." I notice two hockey players slam into the boards together.

"Am I allowed to say that this sport is by far more interesting than our guys' sports?" Piper speaks in a hushed tone.

I scan the room to ensure nobody can hear us. "Hockey totally is."

"And what you said about Spencer. I don't think he is losing interest. He just has Hadley, and I'm sure the closer to baseball season we get, the more his focus shifts."

Blowing out a breath, I turn to walk to the buffet. Piper follows me, and we each take a plate to grab snacks. "I mean, in the grand scheme of things, the only thing that is my hard red flag is when someone lies to me, I've had enough of that."

The sound of a throat clearing makes me glance over my shoulder to find Hudson and Spencer arriving in the room, and maybe he heard me. Spencer just continues to have a wry smile.

Piper walks to Hudson to give him a kiss. "How was it down there?"

"Cold, but damn, Ford is fast and ruthless." Hudson wraps an arm around Piper.

"I'm sure he will appreciate that we're here," Spencer adds.

Okay, I think he definitely heard me, as he is avoiding eye contact.

"I think I'm going to run to the ladies' room, I'll be right back," I announce.

Leaving the room, I can't help but feel a familiar pit in my stomach. A feeling of impending doom.

And five minutes later when I return, I see Spencer talking with my mom. It isn't the "charm the girlfriend's mother" type of mood between them either, it seems to be more serious.

"It's your decision." My mother's voice is the last I hear as they both notice me, and their posture changes. They give one another a confirming look and throw on smiles.

"Everything okay?" I ask just as Spencer brings his arm around me for a side hug.

He smiles weakly at me. "It's fine. The game is almost over. We're in the lead, so we can escape now if you want, before it gets busy."

"Yeah, sure."

"Enjoy your evening, you two. Don't forget to nail down those holiday plans, then we can schedule when to meet," my mother reminds us before hugging me.

Searching for Piper and Hudson, I see they are busy talking with someone, probably my uncle's lawyer. They both wave to us, and Piper blows me a kiss before indicating with her fingers to call her.

"Bye, Mom," I say.

Stepping back, Spencer takes my hand in his and leads the way. Security offers us a different way out to avoid the crowd, and the entire walk feels like something has shifted.

The car ride back to my place is no different, and by the time we get into my apartment, I can't take it because he is what I want, and I thought I've been clear, but that also means I will be shattered if he doesn't feel the same way.

I throw the keys onto my kitchen counter and turn to Spencer. "If you want to break up then do it now, this silence is excruciating."

Spencer looks at me like I'm crazy and steps to me, quickly interlinking our fingers. "Why in the world do you think that?"

I don't look into his eyes. "Because you've been acting

strange. Especially since Hadley upgraded me in the friend book, you've been… I don't know. Something is on your mind."

I notice his chest rising as he heaves a sigh. "I heard what you said." My eyes shoot up to meet his. "About how lies are your red flag."

"And?"

Nerves seem to flood his face. "I've been trying to find a way to tell you…"

"Tell me what?" I feel that pit in my stomach crawl up inside of me, reaching my chest and causing my throat to strain. I hate fear.

"I want to be honest."

"About what?" I feel like I may throw up.

Spencer glances away then looks down at our hands entwined together. "I lied about the video."

I drop our hands like a hot tamale. "What?"

"I mean partially. My cloud was hacked and the video was on it, it's just that it didn't take as long to be solved." I can tell he is biting his inner cheek.

"But you had me stay with you when we hated each other." I'm trying to grasp what this all means.

"At first it was true, but I might have delayed telling you some important details." He pinches his nose, unsure where to look.

I weave my fingers through my hair as I attempt to put the puzzle pieces together. "What details?"

"It was solved already the day we went to Pioneer Park."

I feel my eyes go bold. "But you only said a week later that the situation was solved."

Finally, he looks up at me with guilt flooding his face. "I know. The call I got at Pioneer Park wasn't my agent, it was Celeste from your mother's law firm to confirm."

"Why didn't you tell me?" My hands come up into the air, and I clench my fists together. "I thought for a week longer than I needed to that someone might leak a video of you and me doing something wildly good but totally for nobody to see."

"I'm so sorry. I just… I don't know, seeing you with Hadley, and you were jealous of the pioneer making soup—"

My palm flies up. "Are you kidding me? Do not bring that twenty-year-old dressed in a bonnet into this discussion. What would possess you? We wanted to kill each other that day." My voice is fuming.

"Something inside me just, I don't know… was curious."

Damn it, his smoldering eyes do something to me, and when he steps closer, I feel my heart quicken.

"Do. Not. Step closer," I seethe out. "I will not let your wicked ways break down my resolve," I admit.

I shake my head before I rub my face into my hands. Spencer is quick to grab my arm, hooks his finger under my chin, and ensures I'm staring into his ridiculously handsome eyes.

"Who knows, maybe if I didn't do that then we would never have happened, and I'm so happy we happened." His face is pleading with me to understand.

But I feel a tear form in my eye. "It's not even about the video. In some fucked-up way, maybe one day I will think your ridiculous scheme is sweet. But you lied to me, and I hate lies. Would you have even told me if you didn't hear me making that comment?"

"Yes. I've been wrestling with it for weeks, and with so many other things I want to tell you," he swears.

"Lies are lies. My ex lied to me when he said he wanted to marry me, Hudson and Piper lied to me when they were seeing one another in secret, now you lied to me. I hate feeling like a fucking fool and like I'm some idiot for not seeing the signs sooner." I'm boiling with anger.

Spencer still kisses my forehead, as if it will make it all okay. "I'm so sorry. I promise you, I didn't do it to hurt you. I want to be honest, put it all on the table."

"I'm so angry."

He bows his head, ashamed. "Tell me what to do to make this better."

That damn salty tear streams down my cheek. "I think you should leave."

"Not until I tell you something else that you should know."

Shaking my head and stepping back, I stand firm because I know I will just crumble into his arms. "No. I need space right now to calm down."

"April, please—"

"No. I'm having complete déjà vu to a time where you drove me nuts in all the wrong ways," I snipe. "Please." I hold my palm up to him and feel defeated. "Just go."

His face stills before he flexes his jaw. It takes a few seconds, but he relents and walks past me and out the door.

24

SPENCER

I swipe my palm across my face in the hope of rubbing off my exhaustion. After April asked for her space, I gave it to her by heading straight to a hotel. It was two glasses of bourbon before I attempted to sleep and that didn't really happen.

Now I'm staring at a plate of bacon and eggs, but all I want to do is throw it against a wall.

A hard knock against my hotel room door is maybe welcome, even though it's not April. "Open up." Ford is on the other side.

I walk to the door to open it and immediately walk back to the sofa in my lounge area. "What are you doing here?"

"I always stay in this hotel after a game, you know that. Plus, you sent a *Ford, I think I fucked up* text at midnight. I was asleep and need to head to a team meeting later this morning, but I thought I would kill two birds with one stone, so pass me the bacon and tell me what's going on." He doesn't even wait, he just takes my plate of food off the cart that room service brought in.

Kicking up my feet, I lie back on the sofa and take a

bottle of water with me. "It's kind of a big deal or not. I mean, hopefully, April wakes up and realizes it's a minor thing. I kind of delayed telling her when the video situation was under control, and she's pissed."

"Why on earth would you do that?" Ford is busy chomping on a piece of crispy bacon.

"Okay, I admit that it doesn't go down as one of my finer moments, but I guess something inside of me wanted her to stay before the rest of me caught up. I thought she wouldn't stay otherwise."

It's kind of sweet, surely she must see that.

Ford throws an orange at me, and I'm quick to catch. "Vitamin C, man. You have a kid, and they bring home bugs along with their adorable little smiles. While this is probably something your best man at your wedding may joke about… you literally made her think someone might leak the tape of you two longer than needed. She should strangle you."

"Shit." I growl, as his words are not reassuring. "She also mentioned how she hates lies."

"Kind of goes hand in hand."

"I let her down, I know. But I want to lay everything on the table, and she wouldn't even let me finish."

Ford shakes some pepper onto his eggs. "Do you know what is also interesting about this situation?"

"Tell me, oh wise one, who still pines for his ex from ten years ago." I give him side-eye.

He offers me a stiff fake smile before continuing. "You want to lay everything on the table because you feel a lot for her."

"Fuck, really?" I say, sarcastic. "Because that wasn't obvious."

"Geez, someone woke up on the wrong side of the bed. I'm just saying that maybe you should start by telling her that and then confessing whatever else you have going on in your head." Now he is onto buttering a piece of toast.

For one second, I wonder how his physique is long and trim when he eats like that, then remind myself he burns off a hell of a lot of calories on the ice. My temporary distracting thought, I shake away.

"Well, now I have to find a way to see her again. I texted her this morning, and I'm getting classic April again."

I glance at my phone to give myself another dose of agony when I re-read the messages.

ME

> Hey, I really want to talk about last night. Can I come over? Maybe I can grab breakfast from that place you like on my way?

APRIL

> No. I didn't sleep well. Had a strange nightmare then woke to realize that it's reality, and now I need to find spells to curse your team next season.

> Okay then. I'll wait for our next chat.

Yeah, you do that.

Throwing my phone to the side, I pop my lips and rub my forehead again.

"I don't want to show up out of the blue because she did ask for space, and besides, I need to head back to Lake Spark for Hadley."

"Then I'm sure you will find a way to get her to come to Lake Spark."

"Maybe."

A long silence hits us, and I take the moment to walk to

the cart and pour myself a cup of coffee. I inhale the scent to make me more alert, not that it will change anything.

"I've never seen you invested," Ford speaks up.

I grab a croissant from the breadbasket. "What do you mean?"

"In a woman, in creating a family. That's what you're doing, by the way."

My jaw flexes side to side. "Shouldn't that scare me more?"

Ford stands up and confidently smirks. "Nah, as long as you love her because it's her, not because she is a mom substitute to Hadley. When a kid is involved then you need to close your eyes, and as horrible as it sounds, if you can imagine yourself in the future in a scene without a child, then is that woman still with you? And if it's a yes, then she's the one."

I study him for a few ticks. I know he is speaking from experience. "Yet sometimes you have to let them lead the way and let them go if that makes them happy."

Ford licks his lips and thinks for a beat. "No. You may work with their timeline, but you strike when you need to because letting them go isn't an option." He flashes his eyes at me before giving me a wave with his two fingers on his way out the door.

I give him one nod, but mostly just stand there recalling his words, and I couldn't agree more.

WALKING INTO MY LIVING ROOM, I find my mother reading a magazine with a country house on the cover. She glances up at me but seems to be more interested in the article. "Hey there, how was the game with April?"

I laugh nervously to myself and fall onto the sofa next to my mother. "We kind of… you know what, never mind."

My mother tosses her magazine to the side and focuses her attention on me. "Disagreement or ending?"

"I hope disagreement," I admit.

She loudly exhales. "Over what?"

"The truth." My words cut the air in the room into two, if that were possible.

My mother doesn't blink as she stares with concern. I'm quick to reassure her. "Not that. Something else, totally unrelated."

She curls her lips in, debating what to say. "Fixable?"

"I think so. I'm just giving her some space." I look around for a sign of Hadley. "She's in her playroom?"

"Yes, enjoying the life you have given her, living like a princess with that ballet barre in her playroom." She touches my arm. "You know… eventually you will meet someone whom you want to share a life with, but to do that you need to be completely open with them… I get that." I hear the sadness in her voice.

Because this situation affects her too, in a way that we rarely discuss. That's not what the Crews family does. We do, we act, and move on.

"I'm going to tell April the truth," I confirm.

My mother's eyes water, and she squeezes my arm. "Then she must be the one." The line of her mouth stretches, and she blinks a few times, as if she is gathering herself.

"To my surprise, yes," I attempt to add humor to this situation.

"Surprises are what make our life path," she reminds me. We both understand and give one another a confirming look. Her head indicates to the wall. "The photos of you and

Hadley are beautiful, a wonderful image of father and daughter."

"I think so too."

She stands and resumes her unaffected demeanor. "Hadley only had a snack, so she will be hungry soon. This babysitter situation is taking a little longer than we all anticipated, but I'm sure we'll continue to make it work. And I keep finding dog hair everywhere. Really, ask the cleaner to look into one of those pet-friendly sweeper things."

"Ma." I stand up as I attempt to stop her list. She looks at me with her full attention. "I'm allowed to have someone in my life, right?"

She touches my cheek as if I'm still a boy. "Of course, you are. Now just make sure you don't lose her."

"That's the plan," I promise.

25
APRIL

SPENCER

I really want us to talk, but I can't leave Hadley. I know you hate me right now, but she will only eat macaroni and cheese, but she says I don't seem to make it the way you do…

> That's because you use the box stuff.

It's simple.

> It's typical.

Tell me what to do?

> You'll actually attempt to make it?

Well… I mean… I'll try.

> Great, let's call the Lake Spark fire department while we're at it.

See? This isn't so bad… talking.

> It's texting.

So agreeable.

> You almost had me sending the secret recipe. I mean, you love secrets.

I growl at our text conversation from earlier today. He never responded after that, but it doesn't matter, because here I am in Piper's kitchen whisking a cheese sauce. I faltered halfway through the text conversation, got in my car half an hour later, and drove up to Lake Spark.

"Remind me again why you are here instead of the house next door?" Piper throws a thumb over her shoulder as she twirls on the stool at the kitchen island in her home.

"That would mean extra time with his eyes on me, and I'm just going to drop this off and get right back into my car." I whisk with more aggression.

Piper snorts a laugh. "You drove all the way up here to deliver macaroni and cheese, don't tell me you don't want to hear him out."

I grab a casserole dish. "You know what he did." There is scorn in my voice.

She shakes her head in astonishment at me. "I see it more as he tricked you, not exactly lied. He was able to do that because you let him lead the way, and you didn't seem that bothered about the video."

"Because he was taking care of it."

"And you felt safe enough for him to do so, there was trust already there."

"It's not about the video," I acknowledge and pour cooked pasta into the oven dish. "It's the concept of lying."

Piper slams her hands down on the counter. "Yet here you are because I think you want to hear him out and are using macaroni and cheese as an excuse."

"Hadley is probably starving because Spencer is incapable of cooking," I justify and point a wooden spoon at Piper.

"Fine, since you are doing this all in the name of the kiddo, I'll deliver the macaroni and cheese." She's testing me.

I shrug my shoulder and stare at my creation. "I mean, I should do it. I need to explain the re-heating instructions."

"Really? So you *will* see him and talk?"

Growling a sound as I grab the box of crackers, I admit defeat. "I'll give him exactly thirty seconds."

"You can do a lot in thirty seconds," she deadpans.

I throw her a warning glare and begin to crumble crackers over the top.

"Are you actually adding cheesy crackers to the dish?" Piper seems mortified.

"Yes, it adds texture and flavor."

Piper seems to shudder with slight disgust, and she attempts to reach across the counter to grab my hand, but we're too far apart. "April, you've been happy. At least talk, I know you want to, otherwise you wouldn't have gotten in your car at the speed of light."

"I want to be stubborn, thank you very much." Placing the dish into the oven, I set the timer and then wipe my hands together in accomplishment.

"You're both bickering, not fighting. I understand where you are coming from, but it's not about what happened, it's about where you end up."

I sigh because I know she's right, and if I'm being honest with myself, I miss Spencer, even though it's only been two days since I saw him. I'm sure his intentions were somewhat noble, although poorly executed.

"I'm kind of scared." My admission surprises me. "I don't want it to end, but maybe that desire is so strong that I fail to see a sign that we won't work in the long run. It happened before."

Piper rests her chin on her propped arm with a sly smile. "Maybe you will find the puzzle piece to answer that. Sometimes we only find those pieces by *listening*."

She's right. It's irritating because I feel like marriage and motherhood turned her into a confident wizard.

And hopefully one day, I can see relationships from her angle.

Nervously, I look at the oven timer, knowing every minute brings me closer to seeing Spencer.

EVEN THOUGH I have the security code, I press the doorbell. He doesn't know I'm in Lake Spark since we had radio silence after this morning's text chat.

Glancing down at Pickles under the porch light, I warn him, "Don't look at me like that. You're not right." He woofs a sound.

The moment Spencer opens the door, my throat feels tight, and I'm unable to speak, as my heart wants to burst out of my chest, and I can't tear my eyes away from his that are glimmering with hope, and the white t-shirt he has on only adds to the chiseled-muscle, haven't-slept look. He has clearly had a few days of turmoil.

"April, you're here." A smile tugs on his lips, but he's unsure.

Remembering why I am here, I clear my throat and hold

up the casserole dish. "Well, I can't have you burning down your perfect kitchen now, can I?"

"Macaroni and cheese?" He opens the door wide, stepping aside to allow me to come in. Pickles heads straight to his spot on the couch.

"Yeah. It's crackers, by the way… the secret ingredient, I mean," I say as I walk straight to the kitchen, and I feel his presence behind me, a heavy cloud of mixed hurt and desire.

"Odd, but okay."

I set the dish down next to the stove. "I can write down the instructions for re-heating since Hadley is asleep. I'm going to assume Hadley and the macaroni and cheese was a ploy?" I give him a knowing glare.

He smiles awkwardly and rubs a hand across his short-scuffed chin. "Yet here you are, knowing me so well."

Damn it, so true. Deep down I knew the chances of Hadley having a meltdown today of all days were slim, it's the oldest trick in the book, and I willingly played along.

"I'll head back after I write down those instructions."

"Like hell you are." He's direct and sharp. "It's dark out, and you're not driving back."

"Fine. I'll stay in the guest room. I'm familiar with that room." Again, I knew this would probably happen too.

A long silence overcomes us as our eyes lock and don't let go. We're lingering in an inevitable.

"I'm sorry," he whispers. "Can we talk?"

I fold my arms. "Might as well, since I'm here."

My demeanor amuses him, I can tell. He walks to his wine fridge to pull out a bottle of white. I recognize the bottle, as it's from Olive Owl, the winery of my cousin's wife's family.

"Let's go outside, I'll turn on the fire. It's better if we talk there."

I nod, as it doesn't sound like a terrible suggestion, but I stop in my tracks when I see he finally hung the photos from the photo shoot. "See? Perfect décor for the place." I still when I see he added a photo of the three of us along the line of photos. I want to smile but remember why I'm here. I know he's watching me, though.

A few minutes later, we are outside on the patio with the dark lake ahead. The glow of the fire and light from inside the house ensures we can see one another as we sit on the same sofa, but with enough distance between us. With glasses of wine in hand, I notice how beautiful this scene is.

"How come we've never really sat out here?" I wonder.

"Because we run a risk of you swimming in the lake," he jokes.

I take a sip of the wine. "I guess we stick to the swimming pool, the kitchen, and the bedroom."

"Not bad, but here we are now."

"Why do I feel like the video thing is the least of our worries?" A heavy feeling hits me that in the grand scheme of things, it's minor.

"Probably because it is, or maybe because you knew I always did everything in my power to protect you so the video wouldn't be leaked. Okay, I delayed some information, but it was only because you grew on me faster than I could have imagined, and I couldn't think clearly."

The sincerity in his tone pulls near my heart, our eyes holding again.

"Does my mom know? Is that why you two were talking so close the other night?"

A laugh escapes him. "About the sex tape? Nah, she doesn't know."

"Oh, okay. Guess I can go back to being the golden only child again," I attempt to joke and swirl the wine in my glass.

"She knows something else, though, and I want to lay everything on the line because I don't want to lie to you, because we are going somewhere." I sense that he is about to burst.

I don't want to make this hard for us. "You mentioned you wanted to share something else, but I may have been a *little* hasty in my 'get out of my apartment' spiel," I say, admitting defeat.

Spencer takes hold of my wine glass and sets it on the low table, along with his own glass, before scooting closer to me on the sofa.

"You're right. Honesty is important, and I don't want to lose you, so I…" He interlaces our fingers and focuses on our connection. "I need to tell you the truth about Hadley."

"What about Hadley?"

His eyes strike up and pierce with so much emotion that it spills into me when he says, "Hadley isn't my daughter."

26
SPENCER

Her eyes flick up to land on me, and I sense the shock in her, especially when her mouth opens yet no words come out.

I wait a few seconds to allow her to grasp what I said. My deepest secret that I've never shared with anyone whom I've also shared a bed with.

"You said you shared the same blood," she mentions with her voice rasping.

"I do."

"I don't understand."

I rub my thumb in a circle on the back of her hand. "I'm her uncle."

April's head tips gently to the side, with her eyes squinting with confusion. "I didn't know you have a brother or sister."

A ping of guilt strikes my heart. "A brother... I had."

Her hand squeezes my own tightly, and she waits patiently for me to continue.

"Cameron. My twin, actually, not identical, and we were different in so many ways. I was sporty, and he was into motorcycles and skipping school. The photo I have on my living room wall from high school… that's him."

Her mouth forms an O shape.

I continue, "He disappeared for a while, working in a bar on the west coast and partying a lot. We kind of grew apart, and it had been a while since we spoke, but one Christmas he told my folks that he'd become a dad. Hadley's mom, she was a fling, took off after a few weeks and signed away her rights to Hadley, but Cameron turned his life around. I saw him once after he became a dad, because baseball kept me on a schedule, and I didn't get many opportunities to see him."

I don't even know if I'm explaining this right, it's odd to say it aloud. My parents and I just live, we make no effort to say the words, we just acknowledge the situation in our own way.

"What happened?" April moves closer to me, her hand landing on my shoulder for comfort.

"One week in the off-season, my parents got a call. Hadley had just turned two, and Cameron was on his way back from work. There was an accident…" I feel my throat tighten and bile swirls in my stomach. My eyes close, and I have no desire to finish that sentence.

"I'm so sorry." The light from the fire makes her sympathetic eyes more intense.

"Apparently, he had made a will when Hadley was a baby and without telling me made me Hadley's guardian. To make it worse, we managed to see him for a few hours before he passed."

"Spencer…"

It was a grueling few hours because nobody wants to see their brother give up.

"If I could have switched spots, I would have. He always told me how much he resented that everyone focused on me and baseball, but for some reason, he chose me to raise Hadley."

"I don't know what to say."

I drift my eyes back to her. "Nothing. Just listen. I'll never know why he chose me, but he had an idea in his head that it should be me. I promised I would raise Hadley and be sure she knows who her father is, but he made me guarantee that Hadley would only ever know one father... me."

"Spencer." April's voice is shaky, and a tear falls.

"He wanted to argue to the very end, but ultimately, I followed through."

April hugs me and pulls me tighter to her. "He chose you for a reason."

Taking a deep breath, I note to myself how it feels like a relief to share this. I've been holding this in.

"It's fucked up. I wanted to hate him, but she is the best gift, and now I can't imagine life without her."

April creates a little distance from us but still holds me. "You're a dad, Spencer. A real dad."

"I try." I blow out another breath. "She was young enough that she doesn't remember him."

"Your parents?"

"They had a rough few years after losing Cameron, but Hadley was the light for all of us. Sometimes I wonder if it can be that she gives them a reason to be happy, yet at moments it becomes too much of a reminder. Anyway, they are in a good place now but want to honor Cameron's wishes, hence why my mom isn't here every day. She wants me to be the father that it seems my brother thought I could be."

"Who else knows?"

"Hudson, but I doubt he told Piper, and if he did then she seems to be keeping it to herself. And your mom knows."

April's eyes flood with recognition as the dots connect. "She helped arrange the legalities."

April nods in understanding. "That's what you were talking about."

"Yeah. I told her that I was going to speak with you."

She nibbles her bottom lip before it begins to tremble. "Why did you tell me?"

I move my body to get a better view of her, squaring us off, because I need her to have a clear view of how confident I am that I should share everything with her.

"No secrets. Only honesty." She reaches out to rest her hand on my cheek. "That day at Pioneer Park, for a reason I still can't explain, I saw a glimmer of a possibility of being with someone, not just for Hadley but myself. I didn't… want to let that go."

"But you hated me."

"We bickered, not exactly hate when we both reluctantly agreed to spend a Saturday in a park… together." I raise a brow because I know I'm right.

The corner of her mouth curves. "I guess I didn't put up a fight."

"I don't want to lose you, so here I am, leaving no stone unturned, because you and me? We're worth the chance."

A tear falls down her cheek, and I'm quick to wipe away the warm drop from her skin with my thumb. "Thank you for sharing this with me. It fills in a few puzzle pieces… puzzle…" April stops mid-sentence and seems to be registering what she is saying. "Missing puzzle piece." Her smile tilts a little more.

"What's going on?"

"Piper mentioned that I'll find the puzzle piece to answer my question if we are meant to be together in the long run," she explains.

I'm scared, but I've got to ask. "What's the answer?"

April stares at me for a second, lost in thought, drawing this moment out. "That I'm not going anywhere," she promises.

The last few minutes of a painful reality are replaced with my heart feeling full, and it's because of this woman.

I cradle her face in my hands and draw her to me. "April, I'm sorry. I could have handled everything better, but I didn't want to lose the chance."

"You have a lot to deal with, it makes sense. I was kind of adamant that you were a cocky baseball player who was bad news, until I got to know you, and now you're the guy that I hope doesn't break my heart, which means you kind of have my heart." She's rambling slightly but smiles softly when she speaks her last words.

"Having your heart is good because I kind of need it since I love you." And I have no problem saying that; it's not a big deal because it's as natural as the air I breathe.

April plunges forward to crawl into my arms and begins to shower my jawline with kisses. "I love you too."

I don't hesitate to kiss her, cementing this moment, taking her breath only to repeat and repeat.

KISSING APRIL'S NOSE, I move inside of her. We're facing one another in bed, lying on my side with her leg propped over my hip.

Our eyes lock as our bodies move in ripples together.

The first time was frantic, a mess of kisses and confirmations. Afterwards, we stayed naked in bed and talked about how we will lock away the secret that I shared. It doesn't change anything in terms of Hadley. I keep a picture of

Cameron in the house so she's unknowingly surrounded by him, and I will explain one day she had an uncle. I will honor my brother's wishes, and maybe when Hadley is older, I will re-evaluate, or if there is ever a medical reason that she would need to know, but that's not what Cameron wanted, and now she's my daughter, and I don't want to lose that connection to her.

Last night was a lot of talk and decisions. We ditched condoms and are relying on April's birth control, because we just want everything to be more intimate and committed. All through the night, we've been in different positions, and in sleep, we remained in a tight embrace, and when we woke, we said nothing and let our bodies find their way.

I slipped right into her warm wet pussy, and her soft moan into my ear was the first sound I heard this morning, up to now when a string of sounds escapes from April's lips.

Kissing her to ground myself, I remind myself we are going slow for this round. But her heat envelops my cock as I drag my length in and out, and I just want to get lost in her.

Her eyes close, right before I drag my lips along her neck, tickling her with my morning scruff.

"Oh." Her moan is louder, and I feel her tightening around me.

I hoist her body closer to me, our bodies flush as I pump harder into her, reaching as deep as I can.

"I've got you, baby," I whisper.

"Spencer," April coos, linking our fingers resting on her hip.

"Don't worry, I'll fill you up. To the rim," I warn her.

It earns me a long hum, and her breath hitches from my speed picking up. We're reaching the final stretch, and watching her unravel in my arms while I'm inside of her is the way I hope many days and years ahead go. There is something satisfying about both of us already being fulfilled with an orgasm before eight in the morning.

I'll like it even more if she doesn't shower and walks around with my mark still inside of her.

I hold the back of her neck and our foreheads touch as we both move together. "You're mine, April."

"I'm yours." Her eyes sink closed, and her body begins to quake.

And it's not far behind that my orgasm chases hers.

A few minutes later, I'm lying there, still inside of her, as April combs my hair with her fingers. She places a soft kiss on my forehead before she lies on her side against her propped elbow.

"Can I ask what you say when Hadley asks what she was like as a baby? Or if she wants to see photos?"

I trail her arm with my fingers. "She's only asked a few times. I do have photos of her that Cameron had, but yeah, I hate lying when she asks about her first step or what her first word was. Instead, I tell her that she was so tiny and didn't do much, but when she turned two, then the magic happened."

She gives me an affectionate look. "You know what I think?" she laments.

"That my dick should wake you up every day like this?" I attempt to divert us.

She playfully spanks my ass, with her foot wrapped around my middle. "No. Although, I feel like we will be going through a lot of sheets. But really…" Her tone centers us again into normal conversation. "I woke in the middle of the night, and I couldn't stop thinking about the fact that some parents give a gift to someone else. You and I are connected in that way. We both got a gift in the end. I was a gift too, as I was born because someone helped my mom out, which means I got to experience this life, and you got a gift because your brother gave you Hadley and you're able to be the great dad that you are."

I tilt my head resting against her breast to peer up to see her beautiful face. "Who knew we would have so much in common then."

"We didn't. We definitely didn't know until now, but here we are. We can guide each other, you as the gift receiver and me with the experience of being a gift. You're not alone." April's lips quirk into a fixed permanent angelic smile.

"You're ready to keep going, you and me?"

"Absolutely." She captures my mouth for a soft quick kiss. "The tattoo is the date you got her, not her birthday. I've figured it out."

"It is. Day and month."

She traces my anchor with her fingers. "It means it's also the day you lost a brother."

"But I became a father." She plants a kiss against the numbers. "Destiny," I whisper.

A silence hangs in the air. "Now, if you'll excuse me, I need to get dressed and get pancakes on the griddle. Protein version for you, secret-hidden-vegetable pancakes for Hadley, and the Pickles-friendly version."

Reluctantly, I peel myself off her and slip out of her heat, feeling a loss. "I still remember you standing in the middle of the kitchen with pancake mix and confusion when Hadley ran in."

April flashes me a fond look. "It was crepe mix and apparently one of the luckiest days of my life, but I had no idea." She quickly kisses me once more. "I'll be down in five minutes, just need a quick shower."

"Like fuck you are. No shower. Two minutes."

"What?" She takes the sheet with her.

"I said no shower." I roll onto my back.

Her eyes grow piqued. "Are you already telling me what to do, and I want to argue?"

"Sounds like us."

She giggles and walks in the direction of the bathroom. "Maybe I'll listen. Maybe." She slants a shoulder up toward her ears. "But since I love you, I may be inclined to follow instructions," she calls out.

And I'm not ever going to get tired of hearing that I'm leading the way or that she loves me.

EPILOGUE

APRIL: NEXT BASEBALL SEASON

Tugging Hadley along by the hand, I spot our two reserved seats in a prime location for Spencer's baseball game. I've been a few times now, as a player's girlfriend, but this is a first—bringing Hadley. She's never been to Spencer's games because he thought she was too young and didn't want people outside of Lake Spark to know about Hadley. But when she took interest in tee-ball for exactly eleven minutes a few weeks ago, he decided that she can come to his game and see him in action.

Sitting down, I hand Hadley her hot dog, but she seems too interested in the big screen.

"Do you see your dad?" I point to Spencer warming up with throws to a teammate. He takes no notice of us, as he is deep into focus mode.

Dating an athlete is no joke. He was legit serious about the sex schedule. He can't be too relaxed for a game. And his schedule is at times a challenge, especially when he travels, but I moved into his house a few months after he laid everything out.

Since it's baseball season, Hadley spends most of it with her grandparents, but I'm putting in the effort to see her a few times a week since I got a job as a nutritionist for the school district one county over. Spencer knows his end days of baseball are fast approaching due to his age, which means Hadley can stay with him for every season soon.

"How long is this?" Hadley asks before taking a bite of her hot dog.

"Hmm. Well, it can be kind of… long." Not going to lie, football and hockey have bonus points for shorter games. "But I know where we can sneak into the fancy boxes and get cake."

"I want caramel corn."

"Good choice."

I watch Spencer toss a ball to one of the team managers before he runs a few strides to our area of the field, and he hops up on the fence to wave to us.

I touch Hadley's shoulder. "Look, someone came to say hi."

Hadley waves her hand furiously at Spencer. A few teenage fans are skipping down the steps of the stadium to get to the net fence and speak to Spencer, but his attention remains on us.

I blow him a kiss before the mob of fans blocks our view. It doesn't matter, Spencer has to get back to his team, as the game is about to start.

"These people came here to watch my daddy?"

"Yep. I mean, the whole team, but if you want to know a secret. Psst." I pretend to look around for eavesdroppers and then lean close to Hadley. "I think they came to watch him because he is super good."

"Like better than my tap dance?"

"Nobody is as amazeballs as you during that winter recital dance, but he's close enough."

She smiles with her toothless front on display because she's lost another tooth, which makes me snort a laugh because the fairy sent her a letter explaining that she will now be getting smaller surprises because the fairy is switching to e-pay and it's tax season. It was a ridiculous letter but did the trick because everyone except Spencer agreed one hundred dollars was a bit too much.

"Where do you think my grammie and grandpa are?" Hadley wonders as she focuses on her hot dog.

"They're here. They were waiting for their burgers that seemed to take longer." Spencer's parents are always kind to me. We never talked about it, but I know they're aware of what Spencer told me. Maybe one day they will share more when they're ready.

Spencer and I, according to some, are still in the early stages. It's been over eight months since he showed up on one of my blind dates, and nearly a year since our hotel escapade, but our speed is a winning formula.

Still, I would have no problem if he were to surprise me with the next step because I feel ready, and everyone around me also confirms that I've chosen a keeper.

———

A FEW WEEKS LATER, I'm walking down the hall in the Dizzy Duck Inn. I was told by the receptionist that Spencer was waiting for me in the private dining room, as he is finally cashing in on his private-chef experience that he won at the auction months ago.

I toss my phone into my purse right before I reach the door.

The moment I twist the handle, my eyes are hit with a scene from a fairy tale.

I stop in my tracks, and my entire body stills as I soak in the setting.

The room is illuminated by candles everywhere and white fairy lights hanging from the ceiling. Champagne is on ice in a bucket near the table set with expensive white table linen.

The hue of light creates a glow, which only highlights Spencer's satisfied smirk as he leans casually against the windowpane, yet he is dressed in nice jeans, a crisp white shirt, and a dark blazer.

"What's going on?" I manage to say, but a smile is slowly dragging up my lips. My heart is beating so fast because this doesn't feel like a normal dinner.

He slowly walks my way, his eyes smoldering, and when he reaches me, he collects my hands knowing damn well he has thrown me off.

"This is where it all started," he reminds me.

"You want to make another video?" I deadpan, but deep down I think I know what's happening.

He laughs before walking me a few steps to the middle of the room. "I once heard you like grand gestures."

I tilt my head back slightly. "Perhaps."

"Damn it, I knew I should have gotten the hot air balloon," he jokes.

"Depends. What is this?" I'm not sure that I've blinked in the last minute.

Spencer tucks his hand into his blazer.

I swallow. Oh God. He is really doing this.

He pulls out a little plastic treasure chest and holds it up between his fingers.

I'm slightly confused. "Hadley lost *another* tooth?" I kind of thought we just completed the last wave of missing teeth.

"Nah, but since she isn't here, I had to incorporate her somehow."

Breathe. We are back on track. Breathe.

Spencer is kneeling down.

"Wait." I hold my palm up. "Does Hadley know you are here about to do what I think you're going to do?"

He scoffs a laugh. "Babe, let me do my thing. I have one day off between games, so let me take advantage of that. We can talk logistics after."

I ease into a smile again. "Okay. Do your thing."

"April, to my dismay, you are by far more than I anticipated. The good kind of more. We took a chance, a lot of chances. But it was worth it. I kind of want to make sure that you can't taunt any other man, and I enjoy having you around too much, so I'm hoping you will be my wife. Will you marry me?"

Tears sting my eyes, especially when his face has a slight shade of nerves. Does he really think I wouldn't say yes?

My sight darts to the ring in the little pink plastic treasure chest, then I feel shock. "That's huge, I mean the rock, the ring rock, not your rock."

"Oh, okay, that's where this conversation is going." He still seems to be entertained.

"I'm going to sink when I go swimming!"

"Only if you wear the ring, because you agree to wear the ring, as in you say yes to becoming my wife. Preferably lock in that confirmation in the next few seconds or so, as I'm kneeling before you holding up a ring."

I wipe away happy tears and smile ecstatically before I lean down and throw my arms around his neck. "Yes!"

He slams his lips onto mine. "Good decision," he murmurs against my lips before creating space to slide the ring onto my finger.

Standing up, he pulls me up and loops his arms around my middle, with our eyes locked in a trance.

"You told Hadley once that you wanted a prince who went all out. I figured I would try this."

"Listening to our prince talks again?" I give him a glare. "She's in on this?"

"Not the specifics, but she helped me pick the ring. Something shiny for Queen Sparkly and a promise that she can wear the biggest pink dress there is," he explains and brings my hand to his heart.

"A wedding full of tulle fabric it is," I promise. Then it dawns on me how different this experience will be. I was engaged once, and everything felt like a compromise. This time, I'm with a man who treats me like nothing is an ask, only a wish he wants to make come true, and I want to make him happy.

Our mouths find one another for a kiss.

"Tonight, we can enjoy our dinner, and tomorrow the whole world can know," he suggests. He slides the back of his knuckle along my cheek, and I love the feathery touch.

I squint my eyes. "Why do I feel like the important ones already know?"

Spencer tilts his head to one side. "Okay, so I had to seek your uncle's approval, Piper needed to give me intel on your ring size, Hadley was bursting to tell you all day, hence why she said she was taking Pickles to practice being a ring bearer, and Ford gave me the advice that I should get down on one knee when I asked. So yeah, if you said no then this would be slightly fucking awkward."

I laugh and walk with Spencer hand in hand to the table. "Good thing I wouldn't dream of saying no."

He pulls my chair out, and I sit down. We both get settled in our seats, and Spencer pops the cork on the champagne.

I chortle a sound because last time we were in this room, we were arguing and drinking before we combusted later that night.

"Times have changed," I say and accept the glass of bubbly he hands to me.

Tipping his glass to mine for a toast, he grins. "It was a good night."

"Is that what we're toasting to? We made a video, and it was a good night?"

"An excellent night. The catalyst for us." He clinks our glasses. "And if that's the way we started, then imagine the ride ahead." He winks at me.

"Cheers to that." Because I couldn't agree more.

We're standing outside the front door of our house, and he kisses my forehead. Last night, we enjoyed our dinner and then stayed at the Dizzy Duck Inn, this time waking in the same bed.

But now we are ready to see Hadley and share the news. Piper was watching her for the evening.

"Don't be nervous." He rubs warmth into my arms.

"I'm not. Well, I mean, I'm sure Hadley is excited, it's just that before she and I were friends, and now I'm the stepmom. Stepmoms don't get a great rep in her fairytale books." I exhale a long breath.

"You're more than a stepmom to her. You are the only

mother figure she's ever known. And I mean, if all else fails then just use the dog."

I pull his arm from his humor. "Come on, smartass."

When we arrive in the house, even Spencer stops cold. What should have been Hadley and Piper is now… a large group.

"She said yes?" Hudson is quick to start the question train. Piper tsks him.

"Can we see the ring?" Spencer's mom asks.

"You have a glow," my mother comments with her hands together.

I turn my attention to Spencer and quickly pick up that he had not planned this. Nor does he know what to do.

"Clearly people don't have jobs to get to," he mutters under his breath.

I smile awkwardly and hold up my hand to show my ring, which causes the room to erupt in cheers.

But the noise doesn't deter us from searching for Hadley who is walking toward us. We both lean down to her level.

"I want chocolate cake for the wedding, and pink flowers, and pink shoes, and I think Pickles should be mine now since we are a family."

I try to suppress my grin and instead offer her a serious look. "Of course, whatever you suggest."

Spencer musses her hair before Hadley gives me a little hug that is good for the soul every single time. She also said we are a family now, and it's such an amazing bonus to landing the man I want to marry.

She skips off, and I fan a hand in front of my face to ensure no tears fall because, damn, that was a heart-tugger.

Piper brings me a mimosa, and before long, I'm traveling between questions and answers.

It's a good twenty minutes later when I get to steal a moment with my fiancé.

"I want him back," I tell my uncle. "Besides, shouldn't you be at training camp or something?"

Hudson holds his hands up in the air. "Whoa, message received. Just wanted to ensure he treats you well, do my spiel, and I'm expecting I'm still allowed to walk you down the aisle?" He was supposed to last time around, but this time he seems actually excited at the prospect because of whom I'm going to marry.

"I mean, if you have time." I pretend to be unaffected and cross my arms over my chest.

Hudson pulls me into a side hug. "He's a keeper, April," he murmurs. When he pulls back, he points a finger at Spencer. "I'm still going to be watching you."

"Excited for the prospect," Spencer calls out, unenthused, as Hudson walks away.

Walking into Spencer's arms, I inhale the smell of his shirt, a subtle spicy scent. "I guess we'll bask in this another time."

"It's okay. We'll have plenty of moments together."

We both stay in an embrace as I hug him tightly, and my eyes catch something outside the window. I do my best to figure out what I'm seeing. "Hey, Spence, what is Ford doing?"

"I'm not sure, Hudson said Ford was going to stop by."

I jab Spencer's arm. "No. Look outside. Is Ford with a woman?"

We untangle and walk a few steps to get a better view of outside. It's definitely Ford with a woman. He has her thrown over his shoulder.

"Hot damn. I forgot to mention that Brielle is here."

"As in his first love? The ex?" I double-check.

He chuckles under his breath. "Yeah, more like trapped in his house alone with him until further notice. I think he mentioned something about a fake ring, but you know how it goes."

My mouth drops from the news. Maybe Ford is finally getting his second chance…

BONUS SCENE

SPENCER- A FEW YEARS LATER

Shaking my head, I lean against the kitchen island to watch my very pregnant wife attempt to reach the top of the cake with her piping bag. I'm entertained, as April always forgets that her bump gets in the way.

"Come on, babe, I'll help you with this one," I offer as I wrap my arms around her from behind, my hands landing near her navel.

My head rests on her shoulder as we both examine the three tier birthday cake for Hadley.

"Fine. But, Spencer, don't ruin it. Remember to use a steady hand and gently tease the cake." She hands me the bag of icing.

"I shall treat the cake like a lover," I tell her seriously, but inside, I'm amused.

She glances over her shoulder at me and rolls her eyes before she hands me the icing and carefully supervises my hands as I attempt to decorate the cake.

"It's not every day she turns nine, and we are moving past

the princess phase. She's onto more sophisticated things, so a simple cake with a few colors and sprinkles will just have to do."

I give her side-eye. "This is a simple cake?"

"I mean, of course, I made a fresh strawberry filling, and each layer has a different flavor, but I didn't melt any chocolate or anything." She steps away from the counter to rub her big belly and glances around the living room that we decorated last night. "Maybe more balloons?"

I set the icing down and grab April's hands to hold, giving her a quick peck on the back of her hand. "Relax, your mom is bringing more balloons, and my parents are picking up more drinks."

Her eyes hit me, full of love. "I just want it to be extra special for her. It's her birthday, and soon she will be a big sister. I want her to feel like nothing will change."

My lips form an appreciative smile. "We've done our best to include her in everything, and she loves you. You're doing great." Hadley calls April Mom now, and they truly are a team together... against me. But I don't mind, I spoil them rotten.

A dog's yawn breaks our gaze, and we look down to see Pickles looking at us with droopy eyes. How this guy is still hanging on, I'm not quite sure. I'm ninety percent certain that it's the special dog treats April bakes for him. Or maybe it's the occasional walk past the driveway that I convince him to join me on now that I'm retired from baseball. I have a few ideas of how I will occupy my time, but for now, I'm going to enjoy every moment with the new baby.

"He keeps following me around, like everywhere," April says as she examines our dog.

"That's because he knows my baby brother is about to

pop out," Hadley announces as she enters the kitchen, with her eyes set on her phone that she's scrolling on.

April is quick to shove me in front of the cake. "Hey there, birthday girl," April says with a funny tone. "You shouldn't see your cake until the big reveal."

"It's fine, most likely this party won't happen."

"Why do you say that, sweet pea?" I'm a little concerned.

Hadley points with her phone to April. "Dad, Mom is overbaking my brother."

"I told him that he can't come out until *after* your party," April says, proud with her promise.

I snort a laugh, because nature may have other ideas. We're already two days overdue, yet I'm kind of relieved, as it delays meeting him. I'm excited, but the baby thing is new for me, and it's scary in an exhilarating way. I didn't get to experience Hadley's baby months, just like sharing a pregnancy with someone was a first for not only April but myself. It's brought us closer too.

"Why don't you go sit down, I'll finish my supreme icing technique," I suggest.

"No way, I need to get to work on my spinach dip." April is now agitated, but I let it go, because we know it's an unusual time.

Hadley smiles at me with reassurance before she walks over to the sofa to flop down.

It's two hours later when we have family filling our living room. My trusted neighbors, April's mom and stepdad, plus my parents and a few of Hadley's friends from dance class.

Hadley blows out her candles, and I hope her wish has nothing to do with her crush on Ford's son, Connor.

Immediately, the grandmas are into helping mode with cutting and dishing out cake.

I don't drink a beer because I'm on call for the moment I

need to rush us to the hospital. Speaking of which, I notice Piper and April whispering in the kitchen.

Walking to them, I have to grin. "Up to tricks, you two?"

April laughs tightly. "Always."

My eyes dart to Piper who gives me bold eyes. Instantly, my sight whips back to April and my hand lands on her upper arm. "Honey, are you okay?"

"My contractions started. We may need to leave after everyone goes." April blows out a breath through pursed lips.

"Or now," Piper suggests.

My heart fills with excitement that this moment has arrived.

April looks between us, panicked, and loudly whispers, "No! It's Hadley's day."

"Our boy has decided." I study my wife's face and see that she seems conflicted, as she knows the clock is ticking, but her heart believes Hadley should have her day.

"No kid wants to share their birthday with their sibling. He can't come out today. See, I told you morning sex wasn't a good idea," April scolds me.

Piper holds her hand up. "My cue to leave. I'll take over party duty."

She walks away, and I can only grin at April. "It's okay, it could be a while, and he may not appear until tomorrow."

"You're right. I just…"

I rub her shoulders to soothe her. "We're parents to two now, that means we owe it to both Hadley and our boy to do what is right so they are healthy and happy. Our baby needs a hospital because I'm sure as hell not delivering him in the kitchen next to the jar of your sour dough starter."

"I'm being ridiculous."

"You're nervous."

"Kind of. We skipped all the classes, and all I know is that this may hurt a little."

I swipe her hair behind her ear. "It will be worth it. I'll even throw in an extra push present if you want."

April's lips quirk side to side. "I might take you up on that."

"You should. Now come on, we need to get out of here."

"Why don't we just tell everyone that we need to run to the grocery store."

I snort a laugh. "And come back with a baby? Yeah, not going to fly with this bunch."

She groans as I begin to walk us in the direction of the front door where a bag has been waiting for a few weeks now. I give an indication to my mom that it's showtime, and luckily, she brightly smiles, making no commotion, instead offering me a thumbs-up.

But then April's mom notices and shit hits the fan.

Her hands go over her mouth as she tries to hide her squeal, and Hadley looks up from her plate of cake then to us.

"Were you just going to leave without saying goodbye?" Hadley seems disappointed.

"Of course not. It will take five minutes before we even get shoes on my feet," April states.

Hadley walks to us, and we patiently wait despite the rush we should probably be in.

"Grams will bring you to the hospital when it's time, okay?" I remind her of the plan. Pulling my daughter into a hug, I kiss the top of her head. "You know you're my favorite daughter, right?"

"I'm your only daughter."

"Lucky me. I'm sorry we need to leave your party, but your brother got excited and wants to come out."

Hadley thinks for a moment. "It's okay. You'll just have to name him what I pick."

Glancing to April, she nods in agreement.

"Deal."

Hadley jumps in place. "Yes, I win."

I smile at her excitement. "Save me some cake, okay?"

She gives me one more tight hug before running to April for a hug.

Driving around the lake, I'm beginning to freak out because we're not moving. It's early spring which means today of all days the city council decided to clean up the trees that fell during the winter storms that we had.

"Fuck me, I never want to see another deer-crossing sign in my life," April breathes out, clearly in pain.

"Trees are the culprit for our standstill, not deer." I tap my steering wheel with nervous energy.

"I know, but I've been focusing on that stupid deer-crossing sign for the last five minutes. Good God, I'm going to deliver a baby on this road like a wild animal." A wave of pain hits her.

I rub her back as she grips the door handle. My body tightens, as I am afraid her ridiculous statement may come true.

"Relax, I see they're moving up ahead."

She finishes her contraction and looks at me with near possessed eyes. "Don't tell me to relax. You said that nine months ago and now look where I am!"

It must be bad that I want to smirk, but even in this situation, April keeps me on my toes and makes every second an adventure, the kind I want to spend eternity on.

"I love you," I tell her.

"I love you too, but please move this car."

Luckily, it's our turn to pass, and we're driving again. With a new speed and our route time declining as we reach the hospital, I can only reflect on the many drives around the lake that I've taken with this woman.

"Remember the first night that you were here in Lake Spark and we went to the grocery store?"

"Yes, when I was unaware that you had trapped me here, only to make me fall for you, marry you, and now deliver our little bundle of joy. How could I forget that wonderful drive?" A warm smile spreads on her face as she rubs circles on her belly.

"I'm lucky it's you."

"You *are* lucky."

I quickly glance to my side before focusing on the road. "You were stubborn and standoffish. A lot like now, and that's a good thing, because it's exactly what our boy needs. You're going to be amazing at bringing him into the world."

I can tell she's staring at me, sentimental. "I can only do it if you're with me, so lucky me."

Grabbing her hand, I bring it to my mouth for a kiss before holding it tight on the middle console.

Chances and luck can be the same thing.

That's what we are.

And twelve hours later, we are lucky enough to hold our son, with Hadley arriving early in the morning to name him Ashton Crews.

April and I look between our children, well aware that both of them will break and mend hearts one day, but they will also get to experience the love that April and I have in this very moment.

And we'll be there to watch and support them.

THANK YOU

It's always you, the reader, the number one that I want to thank. Without you then this wouldn't be possible.

Lindsay, Autumn, Sarah, Bloggers, Spotify, Coffee…the list of people and essentials is short but so very important.

My family, thank you for letting me take the leap!

Printed in Great Britain
by Amazon